HUSH BABY HUSH
A DCI EDWARDS MYSTERY

BY
PAULA WILKES

This is a work of fiction. Names, characters, businesses, places, events, locals and incidents are either the products of the author's imagination. or used in a fictitious manner. Any resemblance to actual persons, living or dead, or actual events is purely coincidental.

Copyright © 2024 by Paula Wilkes

All rights reserved. This book or any portion thereof may not be reproduced or used in any manner whatsoever without the express written permission of the author, except for the use of brief quotations in a book review.

To Mark, thank you for your input.

HUSH BABY HUSH

1

Jack Hill pulled his old ex-army surplus coat tighter around his body. The weather had suddenly turned cold, and he cursed under his breath for forgetting his thick woolen gloves. This weather played havoc with his old bones and not for the first time he wondered how much longer he would be able to continue working.

Jack had worked at Longmeads Primary School for the last 35 years, since being discharged from the army. He loved the work but just lately his hips had started to complain, and he found that the work of caretaker/handyman was beginning to get too much. He had suggested, to anyone who would listen, that he could do with an assistant. But his words had fallen on deaf ears.

It was 7.00 am as he crossed the still quiet main road, within the next hour the road would be jam packed with mums dropping their kids off at the school and commuters taking a shortcut towards the motorway. He stood for a moment on the pavement and looked up at the front façade of the school as it stood in total darkness as if silently waiting for the day to begin. He noticed that the path leading up to the big iron school gates was strewn with leaves and he made a mental note to brush them up before the children arrived. This time of year, the leaves could get very slippery, and he did not want to be blamed for any falls or worse still any broken bones.

Fumbling with the large set of keys, that he kept fastened to his belt, he unlocked the padlock and pushed the gate open. The squeal of the rusting hinges made his nerves jangle, and he made another mental note to give the hinges a good dose of WD40.

After relocking the gate, he made his way around the side of the building, making sure that all the windows were still firmly closed with no sign of attempted entry. This had become a habit for Jack since the attempted break-in a couple of months ago. As he walked along the edge of the building he scanned the playground and the outbuildings, to confirm that nothing was out of place. After satisfying himself that everything was in order he let himself into the main school building.

This was the part of the day that he enjoyed most, no children, no bossy teachers and especially no head teacher. Mrs Monroe was a small slightly overweight woman, she'd been head teacher at Longmeads Primary School for the last 5 years. Jack couldn't fathom the woman out. When she was dealing with an irate parent she was as softly spoken as a little mouse, but when dealing with her staff she had the tongue that any viper would be proud of.

"Now my lad" Jack mumbled to himself as he walked into the cosy warm staff room "let's see what I can have for breakfast."

Over the years Jack had made this part of his morning routine, once he had confirmed that the building had survived another night free of vandalism or burglary, he would 'borrow' a nice cup of decent coffee and a few biscuits from the staff room.

This morning, he stood looking out of the window, which overlooked the big, tarmacked playground, as he sipped delicately at his Brazilian blend coffee and munched on a couple of rich tea biscuits.

The trees that stood along the perimeter of the yard always reminded him of soldiers standing to attention as they watched over the children. He had named them the centaury trees, although he marveled at the colours as they changed from summer green to autumn amber, they presented him with the daily task of sweeping up bags full of leaves every day which was a real nuisance.

A sudden gust of wind picked up and scattered some of the leaves that he had carefully brushed up the previous day and left stacked against the rear of one of the outbuildings.

"Oh bugger! Forgot to bag those up" Jack finished his drink and carefully washed and stacked the mug back on the rack over the sink. "Better get that done pronto, or those little buggers will have a good time kicking them all over the place again."

As Jack walked towards the big green outbuilding at the side of the playground he cursed again at the lack of gloves. Stopping to unlock the tool shed he selected some strong bags and a shovel and made his way around to the rear of the building.

At that moment Jack's life seemed to go into slow motion, his eyes knew what they were seeing but his brain couldn't or didn't want to compute the scene. Pulling his mobile out of his coat pocket with shaking hands he dialed 999.

As the police patrol car swung into the school parking lot police sergeant Ted Matthew looked across at the young police constable who was sitting bolt upright in the passenger seat next to him. This was his first week on the job and Ted now wondered if he should have brought someone with more experience. The poor lad looked petrified.

"That must be him" the young police constable pointed across the playground to where Jack was pacing back and forward, his face was as white as a sheet, and he seemed to be muttering to himself.

Ted eased himself out of the patrol car and walked around to the back of the vehicle, on opening the boot he took out a battered ruck sack. After unzipping the bag, he handed PC Carter a pair of gloves and shoe coverings just in case, Ted always thought it was better to be prepared in this job as anything could happen, along with a couple of rolls of police tape.

"Okay let's see what's going on" he flatly stated as they walked across the empty yard towards the pacing man.

Jack slowly turned in the direction of the voices and without a word pointed towards the big green outbuilding.

Ted Matthews was the duty sergeant today and had taken the call from the dispatcher "See what you can get out of him" he instructed PC Carter. From the information that he had gleaned from the dispatcher he wanted to assess the situation alone.

Rounding the building he came to a sudden stop, his heart rate shot up and his eyes started to water. In all his years on the force he had never seen anything like it. Reaching for his radio he issued instructions that CID were needed urgently at Longmead Primary School, quickly adding that he needed at least another 4 PCs to attend now.

2

It only took DC Edsel Jones 10 minutes to arrive at Longmead Primary School. He always marveled that no matter what time police were called to an incident, a crowd of people seemed to appear from nowhere and today was no different.

Glancing at his watch he noted that it was still too early for the onlookers to be parents bringing children to school as it wasn't yet 8.00 am. Pulling into the school parking lot he was glad to see that Ted Matthews was the duty sergeant in charge. He knew that under Ted's watchful eye that everything would have been done by the book.

Approaching one of the young PCSO's, who was stationed at the car park in readiness for the onslaught of teachers and parents who would no doubt be arriving at the school shortly, he was handed a logbook to sign and for good measure asked to show his warrant card.

As he stepped onto the school premises, he noted that there were several entrances to the yard and was pleased to see that they were already manned by other PCSO's. Yellow police tape had been used to section off a large portion of the playground where Edsel assumed that the body must have been found.

Ted Matthews hurried across to meet him "Never seen anything like it."

Edsel studied the older man "No?"

The sergeant didn't answer but turned away and started to walk back across the bleak playground with Edsel close behind him. As they reached the corner of the building Ted muttered again "Never seen anything like it"

Edsel stepped past the older sergeant towards the scene, making sure to keep his distance so as not to disturb any forensic evidence that may be present. He wasn't prepared for the scene that was laid out in front of him. On the drive over he had prepared himself for blood, normally lots of blood, or a hanging, but not this.

Someone had made what looked like a nest by hollowing out the middle of the stack of leaves, which had been left by Jack the previous day. There laying in *the nest* was the body of a little girl. She had been poised in the foetus position; her left-hand thumb was in her mouth whilst the rest of her fingers rested on the palm. Her right arm lay delicately across her stomach. Someone had dressed her in a pure white nightdress and had arranged her long baby blond hair in a smooth plait that had been placed over her right shoulder falling onto her chest. To the casual observer she looked as though she was asleep. Backing away from the scene Edsel reached for his mobile phone, he noticed that his hand shook as he dialed the number.

DCI Elaine Edwards, the only person that ever called her Elaine was her mother everyone else knew her as Eli, had just turned on her computer and was sipping at her takeaway coffee. She was waiting for the computer to kick into life when her desk phone started to ring, its shrill tone interrupting the silence of the empty early morning office.

"Morning ma'am" Edsel struggled to stop the quiver in his voice "I think that you will want to see this."

"Sorry, only just got in, explain!" As soon as she'd spoken, she wished that she could take back the sharpness in her voice.

"Yeah, sorry ma'am" as he spoke, he tried to quell the feeling that was rising into his throat from his stomach. "Got a call about half an hour ago to come over to Longmead Primary School, from sergeant Matthews. It's a little girl ma'am."

Just as DCI Edwards was about to speak the doors to the CID room opened and in walked DS Baker. He opened his mouth to say a cheery good morning but after taking one look at his superior officer's face he tightly shut his mouth and stood quietly whilst she finished her call.

"DC Jones, you're not making any sense. What do you mean it's a little girl?"

"Dead ma'am, the little girl is dead!"

"Oh, dear god." As she spoke she stood up and started to collect her things. Pointing towards the supply cupboard that stood on the opposite side of the room, she mouthed gloves to Scott Baker. "Are CSI on the scene yet? Have you ensured that the crime scene is intact?"

"Dr Brown and his team have just arrived and are erecting a tent over her……" he sucked in a deep breath "over her body."

"We're on our way."

After listening to her DC's description of the events of the morning and a quick call to Detective Chief Superintendent John Collins, Edwards and Baker hastily left the Bournleigh Police Headquarters, which is conveniently situated in the city center within easy reach of the M5 motorway.

During the conversation with Edsel, she had been surprised to hear her experienced DC's voice quiver as he spoke and braced herself for what she was about to see.

Edsel set about ensuring that the PCSO's all understood that no-one was allowed onto the school premises without his express permission and that no details were to be given out, no matter how persistently they were asked.

"Why hasn't anyone reported her missing?" The question came from the young PC who had accompanied sergeant Matthews to the crime scene "I mean she must only be about 8. Surely someone must have missed her."

"Has anyone checked with dispatch?"

"First thing that I did after phoning DCI Edwards" the DC shook his head "But like you say, why hasn't anyone reported her missing?"

Jack's mind sped back to the previous day; he had stood at the side of the playground as the school bell had rung heralding the end of the school day. As the bell rang Mrs Monroe unlocked and opened the big glass entrance doors that lead from the inside hallway straight out into the playground.

Parents were already milling around just outside of the entrance and as the children spilled out of the school, they quickly claimed their respective children before heading back to their cars for the journey home.

Jack thought back to his own school days when there had never been anyone waiting to claim him and listen to what he had achieved at school that day. For him every day was the same, he would make his own way home and if he was lucky would manage to get through the night without another thick ear.

Home had not been a happy place for Jack and as soon as he was old enough he signed up and joined the army. He'd enjoyed his time fighting for Queen and country and at last he had three square meals a day.

Pulling his old coat around him he had started to make his way across the playground, when he caught sight of her. A little scrap of a thing sitting shivering on the bench patiently waiting to be collected by a parent who was always late. For a moment he hesitated and wondered if he should check if she was alright. But with Mrs Monroe's words echoing in his head that he must never talk to the pupils, he thought better of it. Anyway, Mrs Monroe was still on site, as she always locked up at night, so Jack went on his way without another thought for the little girl.

Across town Julia Burnett staggered as she pushed herself up from the grubby settee, which was pushed up against the living room wall. Reaching her hand out to steady herself against the mantelpiece she peered with bleary eyes at the old wooden mantel clock, which stood amongst the other debris that had been stacked on the shelf above the old gas fire that spluttered and flickered as it threw heat into the untidy room.

"Aah, 2.30 don't need to go and get the kid yet" her voice slurred as she spoke, and the room started to spin. Her dull eyes scanned the dirty, untidy front room and eventually came to rest on the half empty vodka bottle that was standing on the cluttered coffee table.

"Just time for one for the road." Swaying as she reached out to grab the open bottle, she overbalanced and fell heavily back onto the dirty settee which sent dust motes into the suffocating air. Clutching the open bottle to her chest as if her life depended on it she raised the bottle to her lips and took a long gulp of the clear liquid "Yep just one more and then I'll go and get the kid."

3

A figure stepped out from behind the row of trees that lined the school playground and took up a position that ensured they were hidden by the shadow of the large green outbuilding. Standing stock-still they silently watched as Jack crossed the open area, noting his slight hesitation as he approached the spot where the little girl was sitting.

Drawing in a long silent breath they willed him not to stop, a slow smile spread across their face as they watched him as he left the playground, without speaking to the girl.

Before stepping out into the light the figure scanned the windows of the school to ensure that all the lights were out and that no one seemed to be loitering in the hallway.

When they were completely sure that they were alone, they slowly walked the short distance from their hiding place across the now empty playground to where the little girl was still sitting all alone with only her thin school jumper to protect her from the cold afternoon air.

"Has Mummy not turned up again today?"

The girl shook her head and tears glistened in her eyes.

"You look frozen." the gentle voice continued "I'm about to get some fish and chips for my tea, why don't you join me and then I'll take you home."

"I don't like fish" the child rubbed her runny nose with a grubby hand. "But I do like chicken nuggets."

"Chicken nuggets it is then" a gloved hand was held out to the girl who happily took hold of it and skipped out of the playground towards the car park.

4

DCI Edwards swung the car into the parking lot, looking across at DS Baker who was sitting in the passenger seat, head bent looking up details on his iPhone.

"I see the vultures have arrived."

Scott Baker looked up from his phone to survey the scene that confronted them. They both knew that as soon as they stepped out of the car, they would be heckled for answers that they, as yet didn't possess.

Edwards eased her legs out of the car and purposefully kept her back to the pack of journalists that were being kept at bay by two PCSOs. With Baker at her side, they headed across the bleak playground, to where DC Jones was waiting for them.

"Are you alright?"

"Yes, thank you" Jones glanced towards the tent where the CSI team were busily working. "Sergeant Matthews has escorted Jack Hill the man that found her, down to the station for a formal statement" turning to face the gathering crowd that had grown by the hour he pointed to a small woman who was standing a little way from the others. "That's Mrs Monroe, the head teacher. I didn't want to let her on site until I had spoken to you."

"Do we have any idea who the girl is?" Baker asked as he watched Dr Brown emerge from the tent.

"No. Jack Hill said he recognised her but didn't know her name" Detective Constable Jones swallowed hard before replying "She's only tiny and no-one seems to realise that she's missing!"

Edwards patted the younger man's arm, cases involving children were always hard and her heart went out to her young DC.

"Why don't you go and talk to the head teacher?" with that Edwards turned and went to meet with Dr Brown.

Dr Chris Brown was a small round apple of a man, his beady eyes where half hidden by the varifocal glasses that he always wore. He was known through the West Country police force for being one of the best in the business. Although at times he could seem frustratingly slow and somewhat funicity. However, he was always spot on with his diagnosis of a murder scene.

Dr Brown stood at the entrance of the tent that his team had erected and waited for Elaine and Scott to join him.

As Elaine pulled on the obligatory white paper coveralls, gloves, and shoe coverings she braced herself for what she was about to witness.

"Good morning DCI Edwards"

"Morning Chris" straightening up from pulling on the shoe coverings she looked at the older man. "Any ideas what has happened?"

Dr Baker stepped into the tent holding the door flap open for the police officers to join him "Can't tell much at the moment. But I would say that she definitely wasn't killed here" he bent down next to the body of the little girl. "She's been washed."

"Washed!"

"Definitely. I can smell something like lavender and her hair looks freshly combed and washed." As he stood, he looked down at the small figure "From her core temperature I would think that death occurred somewhere between 6.00 pm and 10.00pm last night."

Both Edwards and Baker had remained silent until now, neither could really comprehend the scene in front of them.

Dragging her eyes from the girl Edwards was the first to speak "Can you tell how she died? I can't see any signs from here."

"That's the strangest part, it doesn't look as though she's been strangled as there doesn't seem to be any ligature or handprints showing around her neck." The doctor moved back to stand over the body. "I can't tell until we move her, but there doesn't seem to be any stab wounds" he scratched his head, through his coverall.

"She looks as though she just went to sleep" DS Bakers voice cracked slightly as he spoke.

"Did I hear right that no-one has reported her missing?" Brown didn't take his eyes off the girl as he spoke.

"DC Jones is speaking to the head teacher now, so hopefully we will know a little more. As soon as you have anything please let me know" Edwards turned and walked out into the fresh air.

After putting their respective suits, gloves, and shoe coverings into the appropriate bin, the two officers made their way back across the playground in search of Edsel.

They entered the school building from the rear, so that they did not have to run the gauntlet of questions from the waiting journalists.

Following the sound of voices, they found themselves entering the staff room. Edsel immediately sprang to his feet as DCI Edwards entered the room.

"Ma'am, this is Mrs Monroe" he glanced to the woman sitting with her head buried in her hands. "From what I have been able to tell her she believes that the girl is Maggie Burnett."

Edwards sat down next the sobbing woman on the overstuffed sofa "I know that this is extremely upsetting for you, but I need to ask you a few questions" she gently eased the woman's hands from her face.

"I'm not sure what else I can tell you." Her voice came out in a whisper as she fished in her pocket for a clean tissue.

"What makes you believe that the girl is Maggie?"

"She's always the last one to be collected from school. Sometimes her mother forgets altogether" tear filled eyes searched Elaine's face. "It's such a shame."

"When you say that her mother sometimes forgets, is she ill?"

This brought a snort of derision from the teacher "not unless you call being drunk an illness" she dabbed at her face with her tissue "She most probably doesn't even know that Maggie is missing."

"We will need a list of all of your staff, including teachers, groundskeepers, cleaners, secretaries, cooks and any occasional helpers" DCI Edwards spoke gently to the distressed woman "It would also help to have names and addresses of the school governors and anyone that has been employed to carry out repairs on the school over, let's say, the last year." Gazing around the room "Did Maggie have any close friends that you know of?"

Shrugging her shoulders, the woman spoke between sobs "Not that I know of, but her class teacher Ms. Pearce would have a better idea about that."

"If you could arrange to have all of the information that I've asked for emailed to us as soon as possible. Detective Constable Jones will provide you with the email address and his direct phone number if you should think of anything else then please contact him immediately."

After thanking the teacher for her help and instructing DC Jones to get a formal statement, Edwards and Baker made their way out of the school.

"Scott, can you ensure that a full statement including any friends of Maggie is taken please."

"Ma'am, are we assuming that the young girl is Maggie?"

"We'll know soon enough!"

5

The drive to Julia Burnett's home was held in total silence as both police officers pondered what was going to take place in the next phase of the investigation. The roads were difficult to navigate as they were narrower due to cars being parked on both sides of the road. As they neared the address that Mrs Monroe had provided for them, the houses seemed to get increasingly dilapidated. Many of the front gardens were adorned with old vans and cars propped up on bricks. Whilst others were overgrown with weeds. Rickety gates falling off their hinges seemed to be the norm and would appear to be the only source of a welcoming feature.

"This looks like it." Edwards surveyed the ramshackle that greeted them. The paint on the dirty frames of the windows was peeling and the front door had been badly patched up, after what looked like an attempt to kick it in. Turning off the car engine she sighed "Here we go."

It took several minutes of banging on the door to get a response but at last a figure could be seen, through the dirty glass door panel, making their way slowly up the hall.

"Who is it? What do you want?" a woman's voice shouted through the door.

"Mrs Burnett, I am Detective Chief Inspector Edwards and my colleague is Detective Sergeant Baker from Bournleigh Police Station" she paused but after no response "Please can you open the door."

"I aint done nothing, go away" with that they saw the figure turn as if to walk back down the hallway.

"Mrs Burnett, we need to talk to you about Maggie!"

The figure turned back, and they could hear bolts sliding across the door. When the door was finally cracked open, the sight that met them was totally unexpected. The woman looked as though she hadn't washed for a month, her hair lay greasy against her scalp and her clothes were covered in stains. She seemed to be having trouble focusing and held her hand up to shield the morning sun from her bloodshot eyes.

"What's that little bugger been up to now?"

"Can we come in please, it would be better if we could talk to you inside."

Opening the door fully to allow her to look up and down the street, ensuring that none of the nosey neighbours that lived close by were outside trying to listen to what was going on, the woman hesitated for a moment but then shuffled back down the hallway and disappeared through a door on the right.

Edwards and Baker followed her, stopping at the sitting room doorway to survey the filthy room. Swallowing hard Edwards walked across the sticky carpet to where Julia Burnett had slumped down in the corner of the settee.

"Well, what's she bloody done? I'll knock her block off bringing the police to my door!"

"Mrs Burnett" Edwards had decided to try to keep this as formal as possible "When did you last see Maggie?"

"Last night of course, when she came home from school" the woman slurred her words and looked longingly at the new bottle of vodka that she had just got from the corner shop.

"Did you collect her from school yesterday?" DS Baker asked.

"Course I bloody did! What sort of mother do you think that I am?"

"Mrs Burnett, please think carefully are you sure that you went to the school yesterday" pausing Edwards lowered her voice "we're not here to judge your mothering skills, but it is important to know if you collected Maggie from school."

Fear was now showing in Julia's cloudy eyes "I don't always manage to get there" she quickly added "but Maggie is 8 and she is quite capable of coming home on her own."

"You still haven't answered my question, did you go to the school yesterday?" The firmness of the question startled Julia as she confirmed that she had not.

"Thank you for being honest. Do you remember her coming home?"

Another shake of Julia's head confirmed again that she didn't. "But she must have, she hasn't got anywhere else to go" she added.

Edwards perched herself on the edge of the dirty settee and taking one of the woman's hands in hers she gently said, "I'm sorry to inform you that the body of a young girl was found this morning, we believe that it may be your daughter Maggie."

"No, no" the woman let out a guttural cry and folding her arms around her thin body started to rock manically back and forth.

"Mrs Burnett, we will need you to formally identify the body possibly later today" Edwards looked at her DS "Please arrange for a family liaison officer to get here now!" Looking back at Julia Burnett she added "Is there anyone that we can contact to come and be with you" when the woman didn't answer "maybe Maggie's father?"

With a quivering voice the woman finally answered "No no-one" looking down at the tissue that she had screwed in a tight ball in her fist "Her father? I don't know who her father is." Looking down at her hands "I'm ashamed to say that she's the result of a drunken one-night stand. Didn't even know I was pregnant until weeks later and by then I couldn't remember who he was."

As they headed for the door, DCI Edwards turned taking in the scene of total devastation with as much sympathy as she could muster, she added "We have asked for PC Susie Blake to come and stay with you." Seeing that Mrs Burnett was about to speak DCI Edwards quickly added "PC Blake is a very experienced Family Liaison Officer; she will be here to support you whilst the investigation is ongoing." Dropping her voice slightly "I 'am truly sorry, but we will need you to formally identify Maggie" seeing the distressed look on the other woman's face "PC Blake will go with you once we receive permission from the coroner. Please believe me we will do everything in our power to catch the person who has taken Maggie away from you."

6

The incident room fell quiet as DCI Edwards entered. DS Baker was already making a start on marking up the huge whiteboard that was fixed to the wall running half the length of the room.

Edwards stalked forward and took the marker pen from her sergeant's hand wrote in huge capitals MAGGIE BURNETT. Under the heading she carefully placed two pictures of the little girl, one of her in her school uniform shyly smiling at the camera and the second of the child at the crime scene. Stepping to one side of the board she handed the marker pen back to Baker.

Looking around the room at the assembled team she was both shocked and pleasantly surprised to see that not only did the female officers have tears in their eyes, but the male officers were glassy eyed also. To Edwards this showed how much they cared.

Clearing her throat, she began to speak "For all of us this is going to be a very difficult case" nodding her head towards the pictures of Maggie she continued "Baker and I have been to see the mother and to put it bluntly we don't believe that she is going to be of much help to us. From what she has told us last night she was so drunk that we cannot even be sure if little Maggie made it home from school"

"Burnett" this statement came from one of the young PC's who had been drafted in to help with fielding any enquiries that were bound to come in once the public got wind of the murder "Sorry to interrupt but is the mother Julia Burnett?"

"Do you know her?" turning from the whiteboard Baker looked straight at the younger man, eyes narrowing he continued "If you know her you'd better say now lad!"

The young PC swallowed hard and stammered "I don't know her in that way, sir!" looking at his colleague that was sitting next to him "we arrested her in town, what about a week ago?" This last comment he directed at the officer to his right.

"Oh god yeh, we did" confirming this with a nod of his head he continued "to be honest Ma'am, we had no idea that she had a kid. Although she was locked up in the cells overnight to sober up, she never mentioned that she had a kid at home."

Just as Edwards was about to speak the incident room door burst open and in hurried Chris Brown without waiting to be asked for his findings he walked to the front of the room and handed Edwards a plastic incident bag containing a small piece of paper.

"That was folded neatly and had been placed in the child's hand before her thumb had been placed in her mouth" he flatly stated.

'*Otros tiraron a otra botella*' was neatly written in italic on one side of the paper.

"I'm no expert on Spanish but my trusty google translator says its 'another shot another bottle. If you turn the paper over on the back is written 'Silencio del bebe Silencio' again according to google this is 'Hush Baby Hush'" with that Chris Brown perched himself on the edge of the desk as he continued "a preliminary look at the child has shown no outward signs of a crime. There are no ligature marks or fingerprints to suggest strangulation and no signs of the child being stabbed or shot," at this he gave a deep sigh before concluding "we will be carrying out a complete autopsy first thing in the morning."

"I'm almost afraid to ask but was there any sign of sexual abuse?" Edwards quietly asked.

"No. Definitely no sign of any sexual activity" Chris Brown peered over the top of his glasses as he spoke "we carried out a rape test, just in case but that was negative" pushing his glasses back to the bridge of his nose he continued "I am no specialist on clothing, but I believe that the nightdress she was wearing, although very well done, is in fact homemade. The fabric appears to be linen, not sure if that helps at all. We have sent the article to the lab for them to assess." With that he handed Elaine two photographs, one of the note and one of the nightdress.

"Thank you, Chris please let me know as soon as you have any further information" After handing the photographs to Baker to put on the whiteboard, Edwards turned her attention back to the waiting team "right who can give me feedback on the door-to-door enquiries."

"Nothing Ma'am" Ted Matthews confirmed "it was such a cold night that everyone just wanted to get home, no-one seems to have seen anything. We also checked for any

CCTV and doorbell cameras but there are none in the immediate area. Also, the school doesn't have CCTV."

"What about the search of the playground Edsel?"

"The forensic team found a couple of footprints close to the front of the shed but nothing in or around the area where the child was found."

"How did the interview go with the caretaker" Edwards pointed her pen to Jack Hill's name that Scott had already written on the white board "Do we think that he's a suspect?"

"He confirmed seeing the young girl when everyone else had left the school" PC Carter glanced down at his notes "but to be honest ma'am he's been warned by Mrs Monroe that he must not talk to any of the pupils and from what I can gather he would be too terrified to disobey her. From what he said she seems to be a bit of a tyrant and rules the school, at least the staff, with an iron fist."

"Right well we keep looking, she didn't fall from the sky so there has to be something to link the person who did this to her. In light of the information from Dr Brown I need someone to canvas all of the outlets that sell white linen material, including online sellers, any volunteers?"

"I would like to do that Ma'am" PC Carter blushed slightly as he spoke.

"Great, thank you." Looking towards Sergeant Matthews "Ted can you allocate the list of members of staff that the school secretary should be emailing through, I need a full background on all of them please" pausing "Edsel, can you dig into Jack Hills background, employment, family whatever you can find please".

As Edwards turned towards her desk she suddenly stopped and in a quiet voice added "From now on I want her acknowledged as Maggie not the child or the kid but Maggie, do you all understand?"

7

Scott Baker always dreaded autopsies, he always made sure that he was first to get to the hospital which gave him time to compose himself.

Today as he waited outside the hospital's doors, his mind raced back to the time when he had attended his first autopsy. On the way to the hospital mortuary for the first time, where a special post-mortem room was located, he had no idea what to expect apart from what he had seen on TV crime shows and in films.

On reaching the building on that first morning, a sudden fear had taken over him as he had no idea what was about to happen. He had seen dead bodies in a whole variety of different states, but this was different.

After being met by the female pathologist who was going to be doing the autopsy, he had been given the option of watching from outside the room through the glass window or being present in the room when the procedure happened. He had taken the second option.

Whilst putting on the medical safety gown and wellingtons his stomach had started to churn, and he wondered if he had made the right choice. Once he was fully clothed, he had been shown into the medical examination room. The smell was unique, stale air, cold breeze, and the whiff of death.

The body of a white man, early 50's was lying naked on the metal table in front of him. The pathologist examined the body for any obvious cause of death, but nothing was found.

First the chest was opened with what can only be described as a pair of secateurs. The flesh was then cut with a scalpel and snipping through the ribs with a sharp crack until the whole of the rib cage was taken off exposing the man's inside. Each organ was removed and tossed onto the scales for weighing, liver, kidney, heart before out came the lungs. Huge sacks which the pathologist squeezed showing water and the effects of smoking. The liver was ruined due to alcoholism.

Next the tongue. The pathologist starts by cutting way down in the man's throat and pulls this snake-like object out of the body. The tongue is a huge muscle that you can't even imagine inside of you.

The smell at this point is getting worse and the sense of nausea is starting to take effect. A smell like no other, not rotting flesh but stale and death.

At this point all the man's organs get placed into a black bin bag, this is then put back inside the open chest,

He watched as the pathologist picks up a power saw and approaches the head, cutting around the skull until she grabs the top and pops the top of the skull off exposing the brain. She reaches inside the skull and with two hands and with one cut takes the brain out of the skull before placing it on the scale for weighing. After checking the weight, it was put back inside the skull. This is the worst bit, the sound of the saw, the pop of the skull and watching as the brain this watery blubbery mass being handled had given him endless nightmares for weeks afterwards. Thank goodness at last the ordeal was now over.

After taking off the medical clothes, I had spoken to the pathologist who informed me that the cause of death was due to alcoholism and asthma, which had led to a fatal heart attack.

In the car driving away, the stale smell of death still seemed to cling to my clothes and my nostrils but oddly despite everything that I experienced and had witnessed the one thing that has stuck with me over all this time is the size of the human tongue!

As Edwards swung her car into the hospital parking lot, she noticed that Baker's car was already parked and guessed that he had arrived early to compose himself before the ordeal that awaited them.

Edwards always thought it was strange how everyone that she knew had their own system of dealing with autopsies. Baker always arrived early and would stroll around the hospital grounds before entering the building. Jones would pace back and forward in front of the lifts waiting for her to join him chewing noisily on gum, which always reminded her of a cow chewing the cud. As for her own idiosyncrasies she always had to have a fresh outfit in the car so that as soon as she arrived back at the station she could change. It was strange how the smell of the mortuary clung to not only your nostrils but also your clothes.

Joining Baker at the lift neither exchanged the normal morning pleasantries as neither of them were sure that they were ready or prepared to view the body of a child so early in the morning.

Edwards could never explain why she could view a body at the crime scene with an open mind, but as soon as the body was laid out in the morgue her stomach would do a hundred somersaults and she would have to use all her strength to dispel the bile that would threaten to rush into her mouth.

Edwards and Baker stood silently as they waited for the steel door of the lift to close. Edwards pressed the button that would take them down to the bowels of the hospital, where the mortuary was situated out of the sight of visitors. The air in the corridor always felt hot and humid, due to the enormous fans that drew the air out of the mortuary to ensure that a level cool temperature was maintained in the sealed room.

On reaching the basement they made their way along the hot corridor towards the mortuary which was situated at the end of the windowless corridor on the left-hand side. The door to the mortuary was permanently kept closed, other than when a 'patient' was being wheeled in or out by either the mortuary porters or an undertaker. Edwards and Baker took a deep breath as if to steel themselves against what was waiting for them behind the doors.

After a slight hesitation Edwards punched in the security code into the keypad at the side of the door, the door slowly started to open to reveal the cold clinical room. The smell of both cleaning chemicals and formaldehyde was almost unbearable at this time of the morning. Edwards glanced at Baker, she could see that he was trying not to gage, the effect made his face look like it was frozen. Slapping him on the back she whispered, "Come on we can't keep Maggie waiting any longer."

They could see Chris Brown sitting in his glass box of an office at the end of the narrow room. On seeing the two detectives enter the mortuary he stood up from his cluttered desk. The effect of his bulk pushing against the desk sent his office chair clattering back into the wall, the sound echoed around the silent room and seemed to bounce off the shiny steel surfaces. After signing in and putting on the obligatory lab coats Edwards and Baker slowly walked towards where the pathologist was waiting for them. It was clear that neither of them really wanted to be there today.

"Good morning" Chris Brown spoke softly, as was his custom then in the presence of the departed "I have put young Maggie in one of the side rooms. I didn't think that she would want to be with these old duffers" he quietly added as he nodded to two elderly bodies that his technicians were already working on at the steel gurneys which were set up at the opposite side of the room.

Edwards and Baker silently followed him down a small corridor that had doors on either side which were all closed except the last one, this was where little Maggie had been laid out. Chris Brown had already conducted most of the autopsy and had carefully covered her little body up to her chin with a white cotton sheet.

"This is a very strange case" he said as he walked to the far side of the gurney that Maggie was lying on "very strange indeed."

"What do you mean?" Edwards moved closer to the child who still looked as though she was fast asleep.

Taking his eyes off the child and looking straight at Edwards, Chris Brown started to recount everything that he had done during the child's autopsy: -

"Obviously the first thing that we looked for was cause of death, was she stabbed, shot or strangled" at this he took his glasses off and started to give them a polish as he continued "no sign of anything like that, in fact no sign of how she died. Next, we looked at the stomach contents. Here we found a very small amount of undigested food, namely that seems to be coated chicken and potatoes, if I had to guess I would say that Maggie's last meal consisted of chicken nuggets and chips, but that's only a guess" shaking his head slightly he added "we have sent some of this to the lab for analysis and they have promised to give this priority today."

"Do you think that she was poisoned?" the question came from Baker who had been standing as close to the door as possible "I'm just thinking that if you can't find any outward signs of death and she is far too young to have suffered a heart attack or similar then how did she die!"

"It's a possibility and the lab guys will certainly look for any form of poison but from everything that we have observed, I'm not sure that poison is the answer. Depending on the poison we would expect to find some sort of evidence within the major organs, but again until the lab guys have had a good look at the samples, I can't rule anything out" looking down at the little body he continued "her heart, lungs and kidneys all look exactly as we would expect to find in such a young child. We will just have to wait for the results as soon as I know anything I will let you know. As I said it is a very strange case."

8

Elaine stood looking at the photographs of Maggie that had been put on the whiteboard in the incident room. Without taking her eyes from the little girl she spoke to Edsel, who was standing at her side "If only pictures could talk" she stated as she gently shook her head.

Edsel let out a long sigh "I know what you mean. I can't wrap my head around who would do this. After all, if they were angry at the mother for being a drunk and not seemingly to care why take it out on the daughter, it doesn't make any sense."

Turning slowly Elaine made her way across to the stack of papers that had been put on the desk that ran along the side of the room "Where is the statement that was taken from Jack Hill? What about his background?" As she quickly started to sift through the statements, pulling one from the stack she sat on the corner of the desk and started to read.

"Nothing that sends up any red flags. He joined the Army at age 16 and was honorably discharged at age 30 due to suffering a mild stroke. He's never been married and from what I can find has no living relatives. On the whole he seems to live a quiet life, he's either working or in the pub." Looking back at the whiteboard "Regarding his statement from what I can remember he couldn't tell us much; only what Sergeant Matthews told us when we arrived at the scene" Edsel turned from the white board "Do you think that he had anything to do with it?"

Elaine shook her head "No not really, but I think that we should speak to him again as he could have seen something that he believes is incidental and with a bit of further probing he might just remember seeing someone or something that didn't seem odd at the time."

Looking at his watch Edsel replied, "Its nearly 6.00 so he's most probably in the pub, if I remember rightly, he told PC Carter that he goes to the Red Lion on the high street before heading home."

On entering the Red Lion Inn, they immediately spotted Jack huddled at a corner table next to the open fire. Elaine noticed that as they walked towards him, he straightened up and a look of apprehension flitted across his face. She spoke quietly so as not to arouse suspicion from the other people in the bar "I am Detective Chief Inspector Edwards, and my colleague is Detective Constable Jones. Do you mind if we join you?" without waiting for a reply she pulled out the chair opposite Jack and indicated to Edsel to get a round of drinks.

Eyeing the detective warily Jack spoke "I told your constable everything that I know" picking up his glass he gulped the remaining liquid "I really don't know anything about the girl, only what I've already said" looking across to where DC Jones stood at the bar "you don't need to buy me a drink, I was just on my way."

"We just want to go over a few things with you" she held up her hand to stop Jack protesting "we don't think that you had anything to do with the murder but there may be something that you have dismissed that we might find important." Edsel placed the drinks on the table and sat down on the vacant chair next to Jack. Elaine continued "Will you do us the courtesy of thinking back starting from the point that you locked up the shed and spotted the girl sitting alone on the bench. Was there anyone else around, did you hear anything that you now think could have been out of place. Anything at all. Maybe a car that shouldn't have been parked near the school or someone loitering about" Picking up her glass she sipped her wine. "Anything that you can think of could help us with solving who did this to little Maggie."

Jack fidgeted in his chair and took a gulp of his beer "There was no-one outside in the playground only me and that little girl. The lights in the school hallway were still on, so I knew that Mrs Monroe was still inside, and it was far too early for the cleaners to have arrived" taking another gulp of beer "that's why I didn't speak to the little one, if she saw me speak to any of the children, she'd have my guts for garters."

"Why?" Edsel leaned forward in his chair "Why couldn't you speak to the children?"

"Not sure really. I used to have a laugh with the kids until a year or so ago. They used to tell me things just silly kids' stuff nothing serious. Some of them liked to help brush up the leaves and make piles for me to collect, but she stopped all of that" he looked sadly down into his beer "I used to like listening to their silly little stories about their families, never had much of a homelife myself so it was nice to hear what they had done at the weekend or on holidays. Mrs Monroe said that parents had complained about me and that if I wanted to keep my job no more fraternizing with the kids" looking straight into Elaine's eyes "I would never hurt a little one, never."

"In that case can you just think really hard about when you left that day. As I've already said was there anything that struck you as being out of the ordinary" Elaine gave Jack what she hopped was a reassuring smile "Anything at all!"

Jack sat back in his chair and seemed to be in deep thought after a moment "It seemed a little odd that Mrs Monroe was still there, she's normally gone long before I leave" scratching his chin "It could only have been her as she's always the last to leave, she locks the main doors. Part of the cleaner's job is to ensure that all windows and both internal and external doors are locked and that all the lights are off. When I came in the following day all of the lights were off and the doors were locked" picking up what was left of his pint "I think that the cleaners come at 5.30 and do about 2 hours. But you'd need to check that with Mrs Monroe."

"Can you remember what time you left" Edsel looked up for the notepad that he had been feverishly scribbling in.

"Normally I would be gone by 4.30, but that day I left a bit later as I couldn't get the shed to lock, I think someone must have tampered with the lock during the day as it unlocked perfectly in the morning. Anyway, by the time I had managed to get the lock to work, it must have been nearer to 5.00."

"Maggie was still sitting there at 5.00?" Elaine looked puzzled as Jack nodded his head "Okay, thanks for your help" handing Jack her card she added "if you should think of anything else, please phone me."

"Thinking back, I'm sure that Mrs Monroe's car was still in the staff car park" Jack picked up his pint "Well, at least I think that it was her car, but I could be wrong as Mr Austin has a similar model."

"What make and model is it?" Edsel had his notebook ready to jot down the details.

"Not really big on cars" Jack sipped his beer "Could be a BMW but not sure. She always parks in the school car park so it should be there when the school opens" pausing he added "Sorry, as I've never driven don't keep up with models etc."

"Can you tell us anything else about her car, is it a 2 or 4 door model" Edsel pressed on "What colour is it? Anything that might help us to eliminate it from any CCTV we may find."

"Well, I know it's grey, but other than that as I've already said I really don't take too much notice. Sorry I know that's not much help but that's really all I know."

After thanking him for his time Elaine and Edsel made their way back to their car that was parked across the road from the pub.

"What is it?" Edsel looked at his DCI "I know that look, what are you thinking?"

"I need you to check Mrs Monroe's statement, I was sure that she said that she had left the school between 4.00 and 4.15 and that Maggie wasn't there when she left" reaching for her seatbelt "if we are to believe Mr Hill that he left at about 5.00 then something doesn't add up. He's just said that Maggie was still sitting there when he left, so who's not being truthful." As she put the key in the ignition she added "Can you also re-check Mr Austins statement. I haven't heard of him before" Elaine started the car and headed back towards the station.

  On reaching the station the pair went their separate ways with Elaine making her way to update DCS John Collins and Edsel going straight to the incident room to check on Mrs Monroe's statement.

9

The individual paced the floor of their home, on the desk was a pile of newspapers each one had been carefully studied and when no mention of Maggie's murder had been mentioned, the newspaper had been torn to shreds in anger.

"So, one murder isn't enough to warrant even a by-line" the individual thumped both fists on the wall "let's see if two is worth a mention."

Walking across to the bureau that stood against the opposite wall they picked up a photograph of a group of school children all trying to smile bravely for the school yearbook.

Running their finger along the line of children they suddenly stopped and looking closer at the smiling face of one of the young girls and whispered, "Come to me Chiquita." Smiling, they replaced the photograph and walked towards the outside door.

10

The next morning as DCI Edwards sat at her desk studying the crime scene photographs, Scott and Edsel tapped on her open office door. Looking up from the files on her desk she beckoned them in "What is it? You two look as though you're in trouble" she glanced from one to the other "Well, let me tell you that unless one of those coffees are for me you will be" she indicated the tray of takeaway coffees that Scott was holding.

Walking forward Scott placed a coffee down on the desk in front of his superior officer "We wondered if we could have a word before everyone else gets in" he stayed standing "if you're not too busy ma'am".

"For goodness' sake you two sit down, and thank you for the coffee it's much appreciated" eyeing the two men she continued "now what's with all the cloak and dagger stuff?"

"We've been looking over all the information that has so far been collected and it doesn't make any sense. Why would someone go to all the trouble of taking Maggie, feeding her just to kill her? If it was a sexual motive, it would be more understandable, but why just kill her." Scott looked at Elaine "Please don't get me wrong I am very pleased that the poor little thing didn't have to go through that, but it just doesn't make sense."

"Also, why is there no sign of how she died. Dr Brown doesn't seem to have any idea which is very strange. No sign of strangulation, no sign of being stabbed or any defensive wounds and no bruises" Edsel looked perplexed "At present the toxicology department can't find any sign of poison in her stomach contents. What else is there, what are we missing?"

"I fully understand your concerns as I have the same uneasy feeling that something has been missed, but like you I don't know what!" Elaine stretched her back "All we can do is plough on with what we do know and make sure that every single piece of information is fully investigated. We will get this person whoever they are. I won't rest until we do. Now what else do we have?"

"Well, I've been reviewing Mrs Monroes statement, and she did in fact state that she left the school premises between 4.00 – 4.15 pm on the day that Maggie was taken. However, as you know, when we spoke to Mr Hill, he was sure that a car matching Mrs Monroes was still in the car park."

"Yes, but he did mention the other teacher Mr Austin had a similar car, so maybe it was his." Taking a sip of her hot coffee "Has anyone been able to contact him yet?"

"Mrs Hole, the school secretary left a message on my desk answer phone yesterday, but I've only just listened to it" Scott looked a bit embarrassed "She states that Mr Austins extended leave started the week before Maggie was taken." Stopping to consult his notes he continued "however, she said that she believed he had been at the school on 20th September as he had taken some of the students work with him to mark. She's sure that it was the same day as Maggie going missing that he returned the completed marking to the school." Looking up from his notes "she confirmed that he is not due back for at least another 3-4 weeks. Apparently, his elderly mother is extremely ill, and he wants to be with her."

"Did she supply a phone number or better still an address for his mother's home."

"Both ma'am" flicking over the page in his notebook "he's staying at an address in Lavers End, about an hour's drive from here. Would you like me to make arrangements to visit him?"

"Yes. I would like to meet him if you can get onto that first thing this morning, inform him that it is urgent that we speak to him today. Apologise for the intrusion and commiserate about his mother not being well, try to soften the meeting so that he won't feel that he is under any suspicion" The two men stood to leave "Edsel can you wait a moment please I'd like a word with you."

Edsel frowned as he asked "Is everything alright ma'am".

"I know that this is going to sound strange, but can you possibly dig deeper into Mrs Monroes background. Places where she's taught, if she's divorced or widowed, where she went to college, plus if there are any skeletons in her closet, colleges are normally rife with rumors. Anything that seems out of the ordinary." Seeing the surprised look on his face "Just humor me, I'm sure it's nothing but I can't shake off this feeling that something is a little off with her" pausing she added "keep this between the two of us for now." Closing the file on her desk "Once everyone is in can you take a quick morning meeting to ensure that everyone knows exactly where we are with the investigation and get one of the PCs to ensure that the whiteboard is kept up to date. Sorry to put this on you as well, but I need to see DCS Collins before leaving to visit Mr Austin."

After acknowledging her request, he left the room and headed back to his desk in the outer office. Elaine stared after him "Maybe I'm wrong, but my gut tells me something isn't right with that woman" she murmured to herself.

It was early afternoon by the time Elaine and Scott pulled up outside the home of Mr Austin's mother. The large house stood back from the road surrounded by gardens on all sides with a central driveway leading up to the main entrance. Scott gave a low whistle "This must be worth a fortune."

Elaine exited the car without answering and with Scott following walked up the stone steps towards the front door. Just as she was reaching to press the doorbell the heavy wooden door was opened by an elderly lady dressed in a black dress with a white apron tied around her waist. "Good afternoon, you must be Detective Chief Inspector Edwards and Detective Sergeant Baker" without waiting for them to acknowledge this she indicated for them to enter "Mr Austin is expecting you, please follow me."

The interior of the house was equally as impressive as the exterior, with a wide gallery hallway and sweeping staircase, Elaine thought that it reminded her of one of the old movies that she used to watch with her grandmother when she was little, she wouldn't have been at all surprised to see a distressed heroine sweep down the staircase towards them. Her thoughts were interrupted by the elderly woman who ushered them into a very large sitting room. As they entered, a tall thin man stood up from the armchair where he had been sitting and walked towards them. Holding out his hand he introduced himself as Christopher Austin.

Once the formalities had been completed and they were all seated, Mr Austin had asked the elderly woman, who they now knew to be the housekeeper, to make a pot of tea. Elaine spoke "Please accept our apologies for coming here when we are told that your mother is unwell" Mr Austin just smiled at this "however, we felt that it was important for us to talk to you in person…"

Without waiting for Elaine to finish in a very refined tone he stated "I guess this is about poor little Maggie Burnett? I hope that you don't think that I had anything to do with this despicable crime?"

"No, not at all sir. Is there any reason why you would think that we would suspect you?"

"When your colleague said that it was urgent that you speak to me today, the thought obviously crosses your mind as to what could be so urgent that it couldn't wait until I am back at the school."

"Sir, you do understand that this is a murder enquiry" when he nodded Elaine continued "any information however small is important at this stage of the enquiry. You could without realising know something that could be of vital importance to helping us solve Maggie's death." Trying to quell the irritation that was rising in her chest she looked at Scott to continue.

Just as he was about to speak the door opened and the housekeeper wheeled in a trolley laden with a pot of tea and biscuits "Shall I pour sir." She directed her question quite pointedly at Mr Austin.

"No thank you I think that I can be mother today" smirking he asked Elaine "or is that a sexist thing to say? Honestly these days you have to take words out of your mouth, wash them and put them back in before you actually speak."

As he stood to pour the tea Elaine gave Scott a quizzical look. After accepting the cup of tea and carefully placing it on a side table, Scott took out his notebook "Can you tell us where you were on 20 September, please sir?"

"Right here" came the curt reply "honestly officers if you had done your homework the school would have told you that I have been on extended leave since the end of August."

"Are you absolutely sure that you didn't visit the school on the 20th Sir?"

"I've already told you that I was here. I don't like to go far in case mother needs me" he took a delicate sip of his tea "so if that's all you need to know then you've wasted your time and the taxpayer's money coming all this way."

"Actually, we did do our homework" Elaine injected a small amount of sarcasm into her voice "we understood from the school that you were in the area on the 20th of September as you returned with some homework that you had brought with you to mark." Elaine paused to let this statement sink in "So I will ask you again where were you on that day?"

The officers notice a slight blush was gradually creeping up from below his shirt collar, running a finger around the edge of his teacup he seemed to be trying to compose himself before answering "Ah, now that I think about it you are right, I did take some papers back but didn't associate my visit with the 20th."

Scott leaned forward "So can I make sure that I've got this right, when you heard about the murder of one of your pupils you didn't associate it with the day that you were there! Really, I'm sorry sir but I find that very hard to believe."

"Sergeant, I hope that you are not making any accusations that you cannot back up" Looking very flustered he almost jumped out of his seat "I would now like you to leave please, if you have any further questions, please refer these via my solicitor" ringing a bell that was on the table next to him "I'll bid you good day."

Both officers slowly got to their feet placing their cups on the tray Elaine thanked him for his time. "I just have one further question; can you tell us what car you drive please" seeing a flash of anger cross the man's face she quietly added "just so we can discount your car from any CCTV." This seemed to make him relax a little.

"A grey BMW, it's sitting outside on the driveway" indicating with his head towards the window "Now, good day."

On their walk back to the car Elaine asked Scott to ensure that he had written down the registration number and with that they made their way back to the station.

On arriving back at the office, Scott immediately went to his desk to check out the registration number of Mr Austin's car against any ANPR footage available around the school premises on the 20 September.

Elaine walked towards her office when Edsel caught her eye and she indicated for him to follow her into the office.

Closing the office door, he handed Elaine a printed sheet of paper "This is everything that I can find on Mrs Monroe. There doesn't seem to be anything that immediately raises red flags to me" he paused as she started to read the report "Her college courses correspond with her teaching career and the list of schools and colleges where she has taught seem to, at least from the references, be happy with her. It appears that she was divorced in 2018. I can't find any information on her ex-husband and there appears to have been no children of the marriage." Looking down at his notes he added "There was one strange comment from a Ms. Richards who had met up with Mrs Monroe just after her divorce was finalized. Ms. Richards was sure that Mrs Monroe intended to go abroad to teach, she thinks that France or Spain was mentioned. However, she did admit that her memory wasn't good these days and that she might have got Mrs Monroe mixed up with someone else." Looking at his superior officer he added "There's nothing on her work history to show that she went abroad and no gaps in her employment history, so my opinion is that Ms. Richards is mistaken."

"You're most probably right, if all of the other information points to her being constantly employed in the UK, it's most probably a case of Ms. Richards being confused. Great work" Elaine looked up from the report "Thank you Edsel, it's put my mind at rest."

11

    The big black car pulled silently into a parking space just along the road from No 8. Tapping their fingers quietly on the steering wheel the occupant made themselves comfortable for what could be a long wait.

    An hour later the door to No 8 opened and a woman dressed in a short skirt and high heels stepped out. The car's occupant heard the woman shout back into the house "I'll be late so make sure you're in bed when I get back" With that the woman tottered away up the street on her high heels. Smiling to themselves the occupant settled back to wait for the appropriate time before making the next move.

    After a while and checking to make sure that no-one was in the vicinity they exited the car and made their way up the path to No 8. Knocking on the door they could see a small figure making their way down the hallway and stopping behind the door "Who's there?" came a frightened little voice.

    Steeling themselves and putting on as soothing a voice as possible they answered, "It's okay, you can open the door to me, your mummy has been in an accident, and she's asked me to come and get you."

    "I'm not allowed to open the door to anyone "came the little voice.

    Trying to swallow the anger that was building they once again checked the road to make sure that no-one was around "Go and look out of the front window, you'll see that there is nothing to be afraid of" they listened as the young girl ran back down the hallway and disappeared into the front room. Putting on what they hopped was a caring sympathetic look on their face they waved as the little girl peeped out from behind the front room curtain. Mouthing "now be a good girl and open the door we need to get moving."

12

Elaine had just got out of the shower as her work mobile started to ring, muttering to herself she fished the phone out of her bag "Hello."

"Ma'am, I'm sorry to ring you so early but there's been another one" DS Scott Bakers voice trembled as he spoke.

"What do you mean another one?"

"Another little girl has just been found" his voice faltered "Some early morning dog walkers have just phoned in."

Sitting down heavily on her bed "Where?"

"Down near the river, the children's playground"

"Are you at the station?" when Scott confirmed that he was "pick me up."

As soon as Scott had pulled the car into the kerb outside of Elaine's house she jumped in, and they took off for the playground "What else do you know."

"Nothing ma'am, the desk sergeant has sent some uniforms down to secure the area and to keep the dog walkers there, but other than that not much other than its another little girl" his voice still held a tremor "What on earth is happening!"

On reaching the playground the two surveyed the scene. Uniformed officers had already cordoned off a section of the playground around what appeared to be a playhouse and they were now standing guard to ensure that no one entered the crime scene.

On reaching the PCSO who had a clipboard Elaine and Scott both showed their warrant cards and signed in, before putting on shoe coverings and gloves. Carefully making sure not to contaminate the scene they made their way towards where, once again, Sergeant Ted Matthews stood waiting for them. He shook his head as they reached him "I can't believe that this has happened again" he glanced towards the wooden playhouse "she looks exactly like Maggie, dressed in white, hair plaited and a thumb in her mouth."

Elaine patted the older sergeant on the arm "Is SOCO on their way Ted?" he nodded but didn't speak. Looking at Scott she asked "Ready?" With that the two walked towards the playhouse, ensuring that they stayed at a safe distance so that no forensic evidence would be disturbed.

The playhouse was old and seemed to be falling apart. Bending down the two officers looked inside, even though they were some distance away they could make out the form of a small child dressed in white and lying in a foetal position. She appeared to be lying directly on the bare soil with nothing beneath her.

"Oh, my goodness, Ted's right she's laid out in exactly the same way" Looking around "Ted do we have any idea who she is?"

"No ma'am, the dog walkers found her about an hour ago" he indicated to two people who were sitting huddled together on a nearby bench "The lady in particular is very shaken up."

"Did you take their names?"

"Mr & Mrs Carter, ma'am"

Thanking him, Elaine made her way over to where the pair were sitting "I'm Detective Chief Inspector Edwards and this is Detective Sargeant Baker we need to ask you some questions." Noticing that they both looked very cold she added "maybe it would be better if we took you down to the station and warmed you up a bit" pausing she added "my officer can take you via your home so that you can leave your dog there. Would that be okay?"

After instructing one of the PCs to give the couple a lift down to the station, via their home and to make sure that they were comfortable. She told the young PC to ask DC Jones to take a statement from them. Elaine and Scott walked back across the park to where SOCO had just arrived and were erecting a tent over the scene.

Dr Chris Brown was about to enter the tent as he spotted Elaine walking towards him "Have you seen the child?" Elaine nodded "From what Ted tells me the scene looks almost the same as the last one" pulling on a pair of latex gloves "I don't think that I will be able to tell you very much at the moment, but if you hang on and let me take a look, I'll give you a quick update."

Even with her big winter coat on Elaine could feel the cold seeping into her bones, she shuddered at the thought that the little girl could have been there all night.

After about 10 minutes Dr Brown emerged from the tent "As I thought the child doesn't appear to have any visible signs of trauma, but I will be able to tell better when we get her back to the mortuary. It looks as though there could be something in the child's hand, and I expect that it will be another note just like we found before" pulling off his gloves "as soon as I can I'll give you a proper update" looking back over his shoulder "But I can tell you this she hasn't been there long, no dew on her dress or hair, I would guess, and it is only a guess, that she was placed there within the last two hours. Do we know who she is?"

Elaine shook her head "No-one has reported her missing. What is the world coming to!" With that Dr Brown walked over to the evidence bin and removed his white forensic suit, gloves, and shoe coverings.

By the time Elaine and Scott had got back to the station DC Jones had assembled everyone involved in the case and they were waiting in the incident room for her to arrive. All eyes were on her as she walked quickly to the front of the room. As she was about to start the door opened and DCS John Collins entered the room, he walked to the front to join Elaine "I understand how upsetting this situation is for all of you, but we need to keep rational heads in order that these two young girls receive the justice that they deserve" looking around the room he added "and that no other child is taken!" Sitting on the corner of the desk he indicated to Elaine to proceed.

"I would like to reiterate what the DCS has just said, any murder is upsetting but this is especially so when a child is involved" taking a deep breath she continued "I'm sure that you are all aware that unfortunately this morning we received a call to inform us that another young girl had been found. This time the child was found at the playground down near the river. We are at present waiting for Dr Brown to carry out a postmortem on the child, but from comparing the scene to that of Maggie Burnett it looks as though it could be the same person or persons that have carried out this last murder" looking around the room she added "we do not want any of this to be leaked to the press, does everyone understand."

"Excuse me ma'am" a young PC who Elaine didn't recognise had his hand up "do we know who the young girl is?"

"No, it would appear that no-one has reported her missing" Elaine looked back at the whiteboard "just like Maggie." She waited for a moment to let this information sink in and then stated "we do have a photograph that Dr Brown's assistant took at the scene" as she spoke DS Baker pinned a copy of the photograph onto the whiteboard "however, as you can see it could prove to be distressing for some people, so we need to be careful who we show it to. But we do need to find out who she is asap, someone must be missing her."

The same young PC said "What about the school ma'am? Perhaps someone hasn't turned up for school today that could be a start."

"Excellent thinking" DCS Collins interjected "why don't you go over to the school and ask around" looking at Elaine "if that's alright with you."

"Yes of course, grab a copy of the photograph and see what you can find out" indicating the pile of copies of the young girls photograph "report back to me as soon as you can." Pausing she looked at her DC "Edsel, you took the statement from Mr & Mrs Carter what did they have to say?"

"They entered the park at approximately 7.30 am this morning. It seems that they are sticklers for routine. After letting their dog off the lead, they were just walking and chatting when the dog started growling and causing a fuss around the old playhouse. After calling the dog several times and him not coming back to them, Mrs Carter walked across to put him back on his lead. She said that the dog was standing stock still and looking into the playhouse growling and that he wouldn't move. She bent down to see what he was growling at and that's when she saw the little girl." Shaking his head "Poor woman, I think that the scene that she saw nearly gave her a heart attack. I asked if they saw anyone else or if they heard a vehicle, but they said that no one else was around. I asked one of the PCs to give them a lift home and they promised that should they think of anything else they would let me know immediately."

"It's all very strange if Dr Brown believes that she was placed there within 2 hours of being found, the person must have driven there, unless they live close by" Elaine stretched "No, thinking about it they must have driven, you wouldn't chance carrying a dead child through the streets, however close you lived to the park. Can you chase up any CCTV around that area, see what vehicles were moving around at approximately 4.00 am until just before 7.30 am, thanks."

Three hours later Elaine, Edsel and Scott were sitting in her office discussing the best way forward. As no one had come forward to report the young girl missing. Looking through the window to the outside office Elaine noticed Chris Brown hurrying across the room towards her office.

Without knocking the man bustled into the room clutching an evidence bag in his hand "Well not only was the scene the same but this little one also had a note tucked into the palm of her hand" handing it over to Elaine "As you already know I have to rely on google for the translation but apparently 'Senora de la Noche' is 'lady of the night' and the same second sentence 'Silencio del bebe del Silencio' is again 'Hush baby Hush'" he stopped and wiped his brow "from what I can tell it's the same handwriting. However, we will send both notes over to the relevant forensic document examiner and wait for their conclusions. Also, from what I can tell the nightdress is exactly the same, homemade and a linen type of material" running a hand over his chin he added "it's strange but from the stomach contents I would say that this young girl ate the same last meal as Maggie, which was also some type of coated chicken, possibly chicken nuggets and potatoes, again most probably chips."

Elaine looked around at the three men "Well the first note referred to Mrs Burnett being a drunk, so does this note mean that the second mother is into prostitution, or can anyone think of another meaning for 'lady of the night'?" When no one could think of another reason Dr Brown bid them farewell promising to provide details of the autopsy as soon as possible.

As the young PC was about to knock on DCI Edwards office door, Dr Brown opened the door to leave. The PC firstly apologized for nearly hitting Dr Brown before entering the office.

"Any luck at the school" Edsel was the first to speak.

"Yes sir. I spoke to the school secretary, Mrs Hole, who told me that only one young girl had not turned up for school today" taking his notebook out of his pocket he flipped to the correct page "her name is Jorga O'Brien" closing his book he continued "I hope you don't mind ma'am but I pumped Mrs Hole for any gossip, she seemed very pleased to tell me that Jorga's mother was a lady of, in her words, ill repute" reddening slightly the young PC continued "in other words a prostitute"

On hearing this Elaine sat forward in her chair "I don't suppose that Mrs Hole gave you an address for Mrs O'Brien"

Flipping open his notebook again the PC smiled "Indeed she did. No 8 Hillview Terrace" closing the notebook he added "I didn't think that it would be right to show Mrs Hole the photograph, what with Jorga being the only girl not at school today. I hope that was the right thing to do."

After reassuring the PC that he had done a good job she asked him to go and update the whiteboard with the information that he had found out. Smiling to herself at his obvious pride in the praise that she had given him.

"Scott you and I will go and visit Mrs O'Brien" looking at her watch "surely by now she should realise that her daughter is missing. Edsel can you try to find out anything you can with regard to Mrs O'Brien, surely she must have a Facebook or similar social media page" tossing the car keys to Scott "you drive I need to think."

As they turned into Hillview Terrace, Elaine had a feeling of de-ja-vu as the houses were very run down and the whole place looked very unsavory. Turning to Scott she remarked "Poor kids that are brought up around here, most won't stand a chance."

Scott managed to find a parking space and as they climbed out of the car, he nodded to the next-door neighbours house "Curtain twitcher at number 10!"

"Not a bad thing, if Mrs O'Brien doesn't know anything maybe the neighbourhood watch will!" Elaine smiled as a face appeared in No 10's window.

As they made their way through the rickety gate and onto the path of No 8 the next-door neighbour suddenly appeared at their door "You'll be lucky to get an answer there before late afternoon" The old woman called across to them "Can I help you at all?"

"No thanks, we'll take our chances" Scott smiled at the old lady "Why don't you go back inside in the warm dear, nothing for you to worry about" The old woman scowled but did as she was told.

As there was no door knocker, Elaine jangled the letter box flap. After a minute with no movement from inside Scott hammered on the wooden panel of the door. Elaine had moved away from the door and was watching for any movement in the upstairs windows. Scott hammered on the door again and as he did, so a face appeared at the top bedroom window, Elaine held up her warrant card and shouted for the woman to open the door. After what seemed to be an eternity the door was cracked open and the woman from the upstairs window stood there "What do you want?" It was obvious from her demeaner that she had just woken up.

Elaine and Scott both held out their warrant cards "Unless you want the whole neighborhood to know your business it might be a good idea to let us in" when the woman didn't move Elaine persisted "we need to speak to you urgently."

"Don't see no search warrant" the woman stood immobile in the doorway.

"Okay, if you want your neighbour to hear we can spell it out to you here" Scott looked back towards where the old woman was standing at her window.

"That nosey old cow will have a glass up to the wall if she thinks it will do her any good" at last the woman turned and walked away down the hallway shouting over her shoulder "and shut the bloody door."

Once they were all in what past as a sitting room the woman took a cigarette from an open packet and without asking if they minded her smoking lit it and inhaled a lung full of smoke, releasing it as she sunk down in an armchair "Well what the bloody hell do you want, I aint been up to anything" she pulled on the cigarette again "well not since my last court appearance."

Elaine looked around at the furniture and decided that it was safer to stay standing "It's not you we want to talk about, it's your daughter Jorga" Elaine noticed that at the mention of her daughter's name the woman stiffened.

"What do you mean" hesitating "Oh no what the bloody hell has that young madam been up to now, I'll skin the living day lights out of her bringing the police to my door."

Scott had walked across to the mantel piece and picking up a photo turned it so that Elaine could see it clearly "Is this your daughter Jorga Mrs O'Brien?"

"You already bloody know that it is, otherwise, you wouldn't be here" the words were spat out.

"Mrs O'Brien, trust me because we really need you to confirm that this is your daughter" Elaine spoke softly to the woman who confirmed that it was "When did you last see Jorga? Please think carefully it is very important."

The woman lent forward and stubbed out her cigarette in the overflowing ashtray on the coffee table "Last night, when she came home from school."

"Was she here all night with you" sensing the woman's hesitation Elaine persisted "please be honest it is very important."

"I had to pop out to see someone" quickly adding "I was only gone for a little while and she was here when I got back."

Both officers exchanged a look "So what or who was so important that you left your daughter here alone? We will need to know who you went out to meet, what time you left and what time you returned. When you came home you actually saw Jorga, is that what you're saying?"

The woman chewed her lip before answering "I'm not telling you who I went out to meet, that's private and you have no business asking me that." Folding her arms, she leant back in the chair and glared at the two officers and no I didn't actually see her when I got back. I told her before I went out to be in bed when I came home, so no I didn't actually see her" a worried look past over the woman's face "What is all this? Why are you so concerned if I saw her or not?" Looking from one officer to the other "Has something happened at school? Is she hurt?"

"This may seem like a strange question, but can you tell us what Jorga had for her tea last night."

"What the hell has that got to do with anything" the woman lit another cigarette and after taking a long drag on it she glared at the two officers.

"It could be important" Scott lowered his voice "so if you don't mind telling us, what did Jorga have for her tea last night."

"Bloody hell I don't know, she's a good girl and if I have to go out she makes her own tea" seeing the shocked look on the officers faces she hissed "don't judge me until you walk in my shoes. She's a good girl, normally she'll get herself a sandwich. She's not allowed to touch the hob or oven and before you both think that's awful she has a hot meal at school, so a sandwich is perfectly okay for her tea."

Elaine walked over to the side of the woman's armchair and crouching down "I'm sorry to tell you that the body of a young girl was found in the early hours of this morning......" before she could finish the woman jumped from her seat and rushed up the stairs, closely followed by Elaine "Mrs O'Brien please, I must ask you not to touch anything."

The woman stood in the middle of what was her daughter's bedroom and howled like a wounded animal "No, no it can't be Jorga, she's all that I've got" sinking to the floor with tears streaming down her face she looked up at Elaine and pleaded "please tell me it's not true."

13

Elaine was sitting in her office when DCS Collins came striding in "We have been summoned to attend Duncan Fowlers office now!"

"Sir, can I just have a quick word" Elaine walked across to the open office door and quietly shut it "I'm going to need extra help."

"You've already been given all of the PCs that can be taken off of other duties" DCS Collins folded his arms "there is no one else."

"What I really need is experienced detectives, although the PCs are doing a fantastic job that is no substitute for experience." Elaine frowned "I need my two detectives back who have been seconded to burglary over in Evershot." Pausing "Bell and Chambers would be a great asset to the team."

"Well, I think that you have a good point, but I need to run this past Commander Fowler" walking towards the door he muttered "I'm bound to get all the normal bull shit regarding watching man hours and budgets."

An hour later the pair were sitting in a very plush office facing a very stern Duncan Fowler the Southwest of England Police Commander and was someone that you didn't want to cross "So let me get this right, we now have two dead girls, of course I knew about the first one, but no one thought to inform me that a second child had been found! Maybe it's just me but I would have thought it would have been upmost in your mind to let your commanding officer know that we could be looking at a child serial killer!" this last comment was directed at John Collins "But no, it seems that I have to wait to hear it on 'breaking news' on the tv to find out what my own force is dealing with. Would one of you like to take this opportunity to explain your reasoning behind this very strange decision."

John Collins coughed to clear his throat before speaking "In fairness sir we only found the second girl less than 3 hours ago and I have no idea how the media got hold of it as there was no press at the scene" he paused "we thought it best to have the child moved before bringing it to your attention. It didn't seem right to leave her there any longer than necessary. But I apologise for my error."

Duncan Fowler leant back in his big leather desk chair and contemplated the explanation that he had just been given "Right, well maybe now that you are here you could bring me up to speed" the sarcasm that dripped from his words was not lost on the two officers.

Glancing at her senior colleague Elaine started to explain "As you say sir, we have two young girls both seem to have been killed by the same person, but we need to wait for Dr Brown to confirm this" she let out a sigh "Both girls were laid out in the same way, in a foetal position with their left thumb in their mouth and each girl had a note carefully placed in the palm of that hand" Looking down at her notes she added "as you already know sir, the first girl Maggie Burnett had a note in Spanish that translated to 'Another shot another bottle", her mother is Julia Burnett who is quite well known in the area for being a drunk. We have just found out that the second girl is Jorga O'Brien, however we are waiting for her mother to formally identify the body, the note in her hand when translated read 'lady of the night' "closing her notebook she continued "One of the beat officers spoke to DS Baker to let him know that Jenni O'Brien, the mother, is a well-known prostitute in the area and has been prosecuted on several occasions…."

Duncan Fowler cut across what Elaine was saying "Brilliant, so we have two dead children one belonging to a drunk and the other a prostitute, the media are going to have a field day!" rubbing his hand across his brow he continued "we had better get a press release out as soon as possible today. Let's try and quell any speculation before they make these murders into a spree killing," pressing a button on his desk phone "Martha, organize a press meeting for 2.00 pm this afternoon please." Directing his comments back to the two officers opposite him "I take it as read that both girls have now been formally identified."

"Mrs O'Brien will be taken to the morgue this morning by PC Angie Case, the family liaison officer who will be acting as her support whilst the investigation is ongoing." DCS Collins glanced at Elaine to ensure that this was correct.

"You two make sure that you're here, with all of the facts that we need the press to know" leaning back once again in his chair Commander Fowler firmly stated, "I don't expect any more surprises, do you understand?"

At exactly 2.00 pm the doors to the large conference room, where all of the journalists and tv crews were assembled, opened and in walked Peter Duffy the police press officer.

"Ladies and Gentlemen, if I can have your attention please" the room immediately fell silent at the sound of his booming voice. Peter was a very imposing figure standing at 6 ft 2 "Police Commander Duncan Fowler along with DCS John Collins and DCI Elaine Edwards will be with you shortly. At which point a short joint statement will be read. Unfortunately, no individual question will be answered at this time" pausing as a unanimous whisper echoed around the room from the assembled journalists, holding his hands up he continued "I would ask that you remain quiet during the reading of the statement so that none of the important information contained in it is missed. Once the statement has been read you will each receive a copy along with photos of the two young girls. I thank you in anticipation of your co-operation." With that he stood to one side as the three senior police officers entered the room.

Police Commander Fowler waited for the journalists to settle before he addressed them "Good Afternoon, thank you all for coming at such short notice. As you have already been told I will now read a joint statement and I would be obliged if you do not interrupt me during this time." Opening his leather file, he continued.......

On behalf of Bournleigh police I have the unfortunate task of informing you that we are investigating the deaths of two young girls.

The first girl Maggie Burnett was discovered on Friday 20 September and the second girl Jorga O'Brien's body was discovered on Tuesday 24 September. We believe the same person or persons murdered both of these girls, and as yet remain unknown although my officers are carrying out several enquiries and hope that an arrest is imminent.

Postmortems have been conducted but are inconclusive as to how the young girls died. Further investigations are now being conducted by the relevant departments.

We would ask if anyone saw either of these young girls either late on the night that they disappeared or early the next morning to contact us or Crimestoppers immediately.

At this time, we are unable to disclose any further information due to the complexity of the two cases.

Thank you.

With that the three officers made their exit to a barrage of questions shouted from the journalists.

As DCI Edwards entered the office the following morning she wasn't at all surprised to see the team all huddled around the tv which was tuned to the morning breakfast show.

"Okay, so what theory have they come up with" she asked as she took the cup of coffee that one of the young officers handed to her.

"Lots of speculation and hot air from what I can see" Tom Carter one of the longest servicing officers on the team huffed.

"All of the papers, both local and National have the murders on their front pages" Edsel held up a front page to prove the point "most are asking what the police are doing and why didn't we apprehend this person after the first murder."

"Nice to have the backing of the press" Elaine sipped her coffee.

"One channel has interviewed a clairvoyant who reckons that they are ritualistic killings" this raised a snigger from the other officers.

Just as the sniggers were dying down a gruff voice from the back of the office shouted "Well, I'm glad that everyone is in good spirits" DCS John Collins walked purposefully towards the assembled group "maybe someone would like to explain what is so funny about two young girls being murdered, and you lot" he indicated to the now quiet officers "sitting around here on your backsides doing bugger all to find the perpetrators." When no-one answered "DCI Edwards come with me" on that note he turned abruptly and stalked out of the office.

Hurrying after her superior officer Elaine shouted back over her shoulder "Okay you heard the man, get moving. I expect a full report of what has been achieved this morning when I return."

14

As they sat watching the news a smile slowly crossed the individual's face, every news channel was talking about the two girls. Earlier that morning, when hardly anyone was around the individual had walked over to the supermarket and bought a copy of every broad sheet that the store stocked. Carefully cutting out the headlines and stories regarding the murders, the cuttings were then placed within a photo album.

Whistling softly as they made their breakfast their eyes came to rest on the photograph sitting on top of the burau, sipping their coffee they spoke out loud to themselves "At last I now have your attention, let's see what you think of my next move."

Standing slowly and putting on their coat they made their way out of the house and walked towards their car to start their normal day.

As DCI Edwards entered the office she was surprised to see a light on in the incident room. Checking her watch, she noted that it was only 6.30 am. She hoped that someone had just forgotten to switch it off the night before. Her whole reason for being in so early was to try to get her head around both of the murders before any of her team arrived.

As she made her way across the open office towards the incident room a sudden noise, as if someone had tripped over something closely followed by cursing made her hesitate. Quietly putting the bag that she was carrying down on a nearby desk she shouted, "Who's there, show yourself NOW" She was surprised to see a disheveled DS Baker walk out into the open office "Scott, what the hell are you doing you nearly gave me a heart attack."

"Sorry ma'am" he rubbed his eyes as he spoke "Couldn't sleep, so I came in early to try to get the whiteboard up to date" stifling a yawn "sat down for a minute to study it and must have dropped off. The next thing I knew I was on the floor."

Elaine turned away, so that he couldn't see her smile, and started to walk towards her office. Calling over her shoulder "Well, as we're both here you might as well get us both a decent cup of coffee and we'll go over everything together."

Coffee in hand Elaine and Scott stood in front of the whiteboard "How do two little girls go missing overnight, and there are no witnesses."

"My thoughts entirely" Elaine eased herself into one of the chairs and placed her coffee cup on the desk "Why the notes in Spanish? Are we looking for an immigrant or has this been done to throw us off course?"

"The whole thing is strange ma'am" Scott turned to face his superior "How did the person know that they wouldn't be missed before morning, that's what's puzzling me." Scott rubbed his eyes "Is there any connection, other than they both went to the same school, could this person just have a thing for young blond girls?"

Elaine sat back in her chair "Both of these…." She paused before saying "murders have so much in common. Both girls were found in a foetal position with their thumb in their mouths, both had a cryptic message in their hand. The nightdresses, if Dr Brown is correct, have been made especially for the girls and both eat a last meal of chicken nuggets and chips" Elaine stared at Scott "has anyone canvassed the local fish and chip shops, how many adults would have a ready supply of chicken nuggets in the freezer."

"Unless that was part of the plan, along with the nightdresses" Scott stifled a yawn "But I'll get one of the uniforms to check it out ma'am, first thing this morning."

"As soon as everyone is in can you get them all together we need to go over everything again in detail" Elaine sipped her coffee "We're missing something, and time is against us" putting down her coffee cup "If this person or persons think that they have outsmarted us, we don't want another young girl's body on our hands."

An hour later DCI Edwards walked into the meeting room to find all of the team assembled and looking very subdued "Good Morning everyone" a rumble of morning ma'am came back to her followed by silence. Looking around the room she was pleased to see that two new faces smiled back at her. "Welcome back" she smiled at them. "In case anyone doesn't recognise these two" nodding towards the two officers in the front row "this is DS Kelly Bell and DC Adam Chambers. I am very pleased to say that they will be rejoining our team" a murmur of appreciation and several 'about time' were said as everyone in the room relaxed.

Once everyone had settled down again "I have called this meeting as I feel it is an appropriate time for us all to collate all of the evidence that we have on both Maggie and Jorga's murders. Kelly, Adam, I take it you have both had a chance to look at the files" when both officers nodded Elaine turned to Scott who was standing next to her "perhaps you would like to start."

"If we start with what we know about Maggie, we believe that she was taken from the school yard, although this has not been confirmed, after 5.00 pm as this was the last time that anyone has reported seeing her."

"Sorry Scott, but you said, 'we believe she was taken from the school yard' Sergeant Matthews sounded perplexed "Have I missed something, is there evidence that suggests she may have been abducted from somewhere else?"

"No, not at all Ted" Scott continued "it's just that at present we can only assume that this was where she was taken from. As you know there is no CCTV or any firsthand reports of any sightings after Mr Hill the school caretaker saw her. Both DCI Edwards and DC Jones have spoken again to Mr Hill, and some further information has been gained. He remembered seeing a car of a similar model to Mrs Monroes in the school car park when he left. However, on further reflection he has stated that another teacher Mr Austin has a car that is very similar to Mrs Monroes, so he is unable to state with any clarity whose car he saw."

"Will someone be interviewing the teachers again sir?" This came from one of the PCs sitting near the back of the room.

"I have already spoken to Mrs Monroe, and she has confirmed that she did in fact leave the premises between 4.00 – 4.15 as previously stated in her original interview. Unfortunately, Mr Austin is away on extended leave at the moment due to family illness, as soon as possible we will reinterview him to clarify his movements on that day. I am waiting for Mrs Hole, the school secretary, to return my call as she should be able to provide details of when his extended leave started and any involvement he has had with the school whilst on leave." After taking a sip of his coffee he continued "With regard to Jorga we are unsure of when she was taken. We do know that her mother left the house at around 6.30 – 7.00 to meet a friend" a few chuckles from the assembled officers.

"For heaven's sake, we are dealing with a child's murder we all know what Mrs O'Brien does for a living but for god's sake grow up" the look that Elaine gave the assembled officers was enough to quell any further comeback "please continue Scott and you lot pay attention."

"Thank you ma'am" Scott folded his arms "As we know both girls were found in white nightdresses, that appear to be homemade. Both had been washed and their hair plaited, and both were posed in a foetal position with their thumb in their mouths and a note neatly folded in the palm of their hand. Dr Brown seems to think that both girls had been placed in their respective positions no more than an hour or maximum two hours before they were found. It would appear, but we are still waiting for the lab to confirm, that both girls also ate chicken nuggets and chips just before their deaths." Stopping to take another swallow of coffee "There doesn't appear to be any CCTV or doorbell video and no-one in either of the vicinities, who were interviewed remember seeing either of the girls." With that he took a seat at the front.

"Excuse me Ma'am" a young PC held her hand up.

"Yes" Elaine didn't recognise her "Sorry what's your name, honestly my memory."

"PC Cooper Ma'am" the officer reddened as all eyes turned towards her "I spoke to Mrs O'Brien's neighbour, a Mrs Murphy."

Scott interrupted "Ah, the nosey woman next door." Looking at DCI Edwards "You remember Ma'am, she came out trying to find out what was going on when we went to see Mrs O'Brien."

"Yes, yes of course." Looking back at the PC "Please carry on."

"Well, although she didn't see Jorga she did see a car pull up outside the house." Looking down at her notes she continued "She said that she thought it was 'one of that trollop's fella's" flushing slightly "Sorry ma'am, I am quoting Mrs Murphy. She wanted to see if she knew the man, but it was too dark for her to see inside the car. Apparently most of the streetlights around that area have been vandalized, so she was unable to make out who got out of the car" again looking down at her notes "however, she did mention that it was one of those fancy low to the ground sports cars and that it was black." Pausing "She did say that although she couldn't see their features, she was surprised that the person who got out of the car was heavily built."

"Brilliant work. Make sure that everything that you have is added to the whiteboard." Elaine stood "Edsel did you visit the local half houses?"

"Yes ma'am" Edsel looked at his notes "I spoke to Don Vincent, the halfway house manager, he confirmed that the only people staying there at present were both in their early eighties and were recovering alcoholics" he looked down at his notes "however he did contact the Brightstone halfway house, but they also confirmed that they only take women and not men."

"Thank you. Who was responsible for collating information on local sex offenders?"

A hand shot up from one of the uniform officers "I have looked through all of the recent sex offender prisoners released from prison ma'am, none of these are situated in this area. I have also looked through known offenders who have family in the area, but again none of these are in the area, or they are either living in other parts of the country or banged up again."

"Okay. Great work. Who was responsible for visiting the local fish and chip shops and takeaway premises?"

Another uniformed officer put his hand up "I visited all of them ma'am" he opened his notebook "no one could remember serving anyone with chicken nuggets. However, Mr McKeith the owner of 'Frying Tonight' confirmed that he had been away and that his son Trevor had been running the shop for the last month. He was going to check with him and let me know."

"Get back to him today please."

"We've received the report back from SOCO, scenes of crime officers, as they have finished the sweep of Mrs O'Brien's home, the only fingerprints found belonged to either Jorga or her mother. They did, however, find Jorga's school bag thrown on the floor in her bedroom, which proves that she must have arrived home on the 24th. But there was no school uniform or coat found in either the bedroom or the house." Looking down at his notes "However, I have picked up a message from Angie Case, Mrs O'Brien's family liaison officer, she has told me that the person Mrs O'Brien went out to meet was Mr Stanley Johnson" pausing for effect "The one and only Mayor of Bournleigh. Not only that but she says that they always meet at The Olympus Hotel over in Greenfields. I have left several messages for Mr Johnson, but he hasn't returned my calls."

"Really, this is going to put the cat amongst the pigeons" Elaine tried to keep a straight face "Right, leave one final message for him stating that I want to speak to him urgently and that if he doesn't come to the station immediately we will be forced to pay him a visit at home" nodding at Edsel "As he's married I don't think that he will want us to question him about his little liaison with Mrs O'Brien in front of his wife, do you?" pausing "Get in touch with the hotel and see if they have any CCTV that show the two arriving on the 24 th"

"Already on it Ma'am" Edsel smiled "the manager has promised to send it over by close of play today."

Whilst Scott updated the whiteboard with PC Cooper, Elaine asked, "Does anyone else have anything to add or any thoughts that might be pertinent to this." When no one replied she dismissed them with a warning "No one is to talk to the press or discuss anything to do with this investigation with anyone not included in the team."

16

As Elaine walked back to her office she wondered how long it would be before she received an irate call from John Collins or Duncan Fowler, she didn't have to wait long.

"What the hell are you playing at?" Duncan Fowlers angry voice shouted down the phone at her "I've just had the mayor on the phone telling me that one of your DCs has left a message instructing him to come to the station. You had better have a very good reason for this DCI Edwards!"

Taking a deep breath and keeping her voice as steady as she could "Sir, we have information that the mayor may be able to help us with our enquiries."

"What bloody information is this and why wasn't I informed of it before sending out ultimatums to the mayor?"

"We have been told that on the night of the 24th Mr Johnson was….." pausing to find the right word "entertaining Mrs O'Brien, Sir."

"So, what if he was!" Elaine could hear him take a sharp intake of breath as the penny dropped "Are you seriously telling me that Stanley" quickly correcting himself "I mean the mayor was with a prostitute!"

"I can't confirm that at the moment, which is why we need to speak to him urgently. If he was he may have vital information regarding the murder."

"I hope that you are not insinuating that he has anything to do with that" his tone had changed from angry to almost threatening "If, and I mean if he was where you say this could mean not only the end of his career but also his marriage" pausing "remember that the mayor has been a very good friend to the police, and we don't want to sully that connection over some slight misdemeanor, do we?"

Elaine could hardly contain her anger "I'm sorry sir but I don't feel that anyone should be overlooked whilst investigating the death of a child. It shouldn't matter who they are friends with, if they may have information that will help us bring the perpetrator to book then I would be willing to interview the King, if that was necessary."

"Yes, yes of course" Police Commander Fowler started to quickly back pedal "Please don't take this the wrong way, I am not suggesting that we should overlook anyone but in certain circumstances I believe the softly softly approach is better." Elaine could tell from his tone that she had won her case "I will of course leave this matter to you DCI Edwards, but I need to know the outcome of your interview with the mayor as soon as you have finished" after assuring him that she understood the police commander hung up the phone.

An hour later as Elaine was about to bite into her sandwich, that Scott had thoughtfully placed in front of her, her desk phone rang "DCI Edwards, I have the mayor and his solicitor Mr Hardington-Smyth, here to see you." With a slight chuckle desk sergeant Matt Palmer added "We've put them in interview room 2. Just to warn you he's not exactly the happy Chappy that we normally see in the papers, spitting fire and blood would better describe him today. Best of luck, you're going to need it."

Picking up her folder she walked through to the main office "Scott, I need you to come with me, but first can you pull off a mugshot of Mrs O'Brien, let's see if our esteemed mayor recognises her."

As the two officers made their way out of the main office and down the stairs to the interview rooms "Do you think that he's going to admit being with her?"

Elaine laughed "I bet old Hardington-Smyth has a statement already in his sticky little hand" as they arrived at interview room 2 they could hear the hum of low voices from within "Well here we go; I'll take bets that other than the statement it will be a no comment interview."

The room suddenly fell silent as the officers entered and seated themselves opposite the two men "Good afternoon Mr Johnson, Mr Hardington-Smyth, I am Detective Chief Inspector Edwards, and this is my colleague Detective Sergeant Baker." When no reply was forthcoming Elaine continued "Thank you for making the time to come in to see us, we do appreciate your co-operation……."

Before she could finish "I would appreciate your respect in addressing me as mayor Johnson."

At this his solicitor indicated for him to remain silent "Before you say anything else Detective Chief Inspector I would like to inform you that my client has prepared a statement which I will read to you, but other than that he is not prepared to answer any further questions at this time." Taking a single sheet of paper from the folder that he was holding he started to read: -

This statement is prepared by Giles Hardington-Smyth of solicitors Hardington-Smyth and Cross for our client Stanley Johnson.

Our client Mr Stanley Johnson refutes any claim that he has or has had whether presently or in the past any association with a lady named Mrs Jenni O'Brien.

Our client therefore declines to answer any questions with regard to this matter.

Sliding a copy of the statement across the table to Elaine the solicitor indicated to his client that they should leave. As both men started to stand "Please remain seated, I still have some questions that I would like to ask." Seeing a flash of anger cross the solicitors face "It will be up to your client if he answers or not, but I still need to ask." After waiting for them to sit, Elaine slid the photograph that Scott had downloaded towards Mr Johnson "Do you know this woman?" seeing the sudden flush start to creep up from below his shirt collar "We have it on good authority that on the night or early evening of 24th September, that you and this lady were together" looking straight at the man "can you confirm if our information is correct."

"Detective Chief Inspector I have already stated that my client will not be answering any questions, you have the statement............."

Without waiting for the solicitor to finish Elaine slid another photograph across the table "I believe that this is you and Mrs O'Brien standing in the reception of The Olympus Hotel in Greenfields, as you will see from the date stamp from the hotels CCTV this was in fact 6.20 pm on the 24th of September 2023."

"Well, if you already know that I was with her, why the bloody hell are you wasting my time!"

"This sir, is a murder enquiry….."

"Now just one moment, I hope that you are not implying that my client had anything to do with a murder, if so I must strongly protest." Elaine noticed that after seeing the photograph from the hotel that some of the solicitor's bluster had diminished.

"Not at all. The reason for asking mayor Johnson to speak to us is to ascertain where and at what time he picked up and later dropped off Mrs O'Brien. We need to know how long her daughter was in the house on her own and if mayor Johnson noticed anything out of the ordinary."

"For god's sake, do you really think that I would go and pick her up" he looked as though he was about to explode "yes why not, I like to drive around the city where everyone knows me with a hooker in the car." Taking a handkerchief out of his top pocket he mopped his brow "I meet her at the hotel in Greenfields. Normally I go in on my own to check in but that night the silly cow followed me in as she wanted to use the lady's room."

Scott leaned forward "Normally, you said normally you go in alone."

"No comment"

Scott pressed ahead "Sir, this is important, if it is a regular liaison and your meeting takes place at the same time each week, someone could have been watching the two of you over the past few weeks, to gauge the times and duration of your meetings. This would give them a timeline for when Jorga would be at home alone and provide an excellent chance to snatch Jorga knowing that it would be safe to do so." When the man still didn't answer "Please Sir, we don't care how many Mrs O'Brien's you see, but we do care about catching this killer before another innocent child is taken."

Looking down at his hands "Yes, yes alright we used to meet every two weeks." Looking from one officer to the other "you have to understand my wife is a very difficult woman and if she should hear any of this my life would be over." Sniffing he continued "I have never been anywhere near her home and wouldn't know her daughter if she was standing in front of me. I really don't think that I can be of any further help."

"Thank you for your honesty" Elaine went to stand "but just one final point what time did Mrs O'Brien leave the hotel?"

"I'm not really sure, when I woke up I think it was about 7.30 am she was gone."

After confirming that this information would be kept confidential, the two men were escorted out of the building.

On their walk back up to the top floor of the building Scott was unusually quiet "Penny for your thoughts" Elaine nudged the younger officer's arm "what's going on inside that head."

"Just thinking about that poor kid" stopping on the landing between floors "gets home from school, no tea ready for her and the mother so hung up on meeting him that she doesn't even know that the girls missing until we turn up." Scuffing his shoe on the concrete floor "Why have kids if you don't want to be bothered with them."

"I know what you mean, but unfortunately we can't change that" Elaine started to walk up the next flight of stairs "However, what we can do is get the bastard who killed her."

17

Although the clock on the mantlepiece read 12.05 am, the next nightdress needed to be finished.

After travelling miles away from home and only using cash to purchase the white linen material, thus ensuring that no one would be able to trace the transaction back to them they wanted to be sure that when the time was right the nightdress would be ready.

Holding the garment up to finally inspect it, they smiled "Oh, my little darling what fun we will have." Walking over to the desk that sat in the corner of the room they slowly picked up the framed school photograph that held pride of place on the top of the desk. Running a finger along the rows of children they started to recite "Eeny meeny miny mo., who will be the next to go." Smiling to themselves they whispered "Which one of you deserves my very special attention." After studying the photograph for a few minutes "Ah, there you are my little beauty." With that the nightdress was carefully folded and placed in the bottom drawer of the desk.

18

"Morning Ma'am" DS Kelly Bell stood in the open office door holding two take out cups of coffee "I thought that a decent coffee wouldn't go a miss." Walking into the office she placed one cup in front of DCI Edwards.

"Thanks Kelly" Elaine pulled the cup towards her and indicated for the officer to sit down.

"I've been looking through the files for both of the girls and trying to find a common link that fits both murders" stopping to sip her coffee "the only thing that is apparent at the moment is that they both attended the same school. There doesn't seem to be any other common factor, no clubs that they both went to and no shared friends." Taking her notebook from her jacket pocket "in fact it's really sad to say that it appears little Maggie didn't really have any friends, from the statement taken from her teacher it seems that Maggie was very much a loner whether through her own choice or not isn't clear. Although it appears that despite her home life Maggie was a very bright kid and excelled at Math's in particular"

"What about Jorga?"

"Again, I only have what is in the statement, but it seems that Jorga had quite a group of friends, however she didn't do well in her lessons and from what the teacher has said was very often and easily distracted." Taking another sip of her coffee "Adam is looking back through the CCTV, although there isn't any for the immediate area where either girl was taken so he's looking at the major roads around the town to see if he can spot a dark sports car or similar that was travelling anywhere near the area of Jorga's home on the early evening of the 24 th."

"I have this feeling in my gut that we are missing something that is staring us in the face" cradling her coffee cup in both hands Elaine added "I just can't get the thought out of my mind."

"I know what you mean, on reading through the files I got exactly the same feeling. I don't understand why anyone would take two girls if there is no sexual motive. Both murders are strange, the fact that the perpetrator washes not only their bodies but also their hair and takes the time to plait it. Then there's the, what we think, is homemade nightdresses." Shaking her head slightly "and what's with the pose, both in a foetal position thumb in mouths and the note. Do you think that we are looking for an immigrant or is the note put there to send us on a wild goose chase?"

"None of it makes any sense, on the one hand due to the care taken with the girls both before and after death I have started to wonder if it could be a woman, but they would have to be quite strong to be able to carry the child to their final resting place as neither site was accessible with a vehicle."

"So, it could be that we're not looking for one but two people working together, is that what you're thinking?"

"It's definitely a possibility." Glancing through the window into the outer office "We need to know who both girls trusted enough that they would go with them without making any fuss. Jorga, for example must have gone quietly as that neighbour of theirs would most definitely have heard any argument or raised voices and she heard nothing nor saw anything after the car drew up."

"That's surprising don't you think, for someone like that not to stay looking out to see if the person went inside or left immediately either alone or with someone from the house" Kelly scratched her head "after all I would have thought that she would have wanted to know every detail of who it was and how long they were at the house, it's the next day's gossip for someone like that, isn't it?"

"You know you have a very good point. Take Adam with you and reinterview her, perhaps speaking to someone different will jog her memory." Elaine leant back in her chair "Great work, keep plugging away" as Kelly stood Elaine added "It's great to have you both back."

"Thank you Ma'am, it's great to be back."

An hour later Kelly and Adam turned into Hillview Terrace "Christ, what a dump" Adam gave a low whistle "can you imagine trying to bring a child up here?"

Keeping her eyes on the road Kelly tutted "I forgot how much of a snob you are" glancing at him "not everyone was born with a silver spoon in their mouths, us poor lower-class peasants have to put up with any old roof over our heads." Pulling the car into a space a few doors down from Mrs Murphys home, she turned to look at him "Now remember be nice."

As they both exited the car and started to walk back up the street they became aware that their progress was being watched, glancing around several net curtains suddenly fell back into place. "Well, they obviously have a good neighbourhood watch system in the street" Adam whispered to his colleague "Strange though that no-one saw anything on the night young Jorga went missing!"

They had only got halfway up the front path when Mrs Murphy's door flew open "I'm not buying anything and if your Jehovah's you can save your breath and bugger off."

"Mrs Murphy? I'm Detective Sergeant Bell and this is Detective Constable Chambers, we would like to go over a few details with you if you can spare us a moment."

The old woman peered up and down the street from her elevated position on the step leading into her home and when she was satisfied that enough people had noticed that she had visitors she stepped back and ushered the two officers into the hallway.

"I suppose this is about the young lass" she indicated with her thumb towards the adjoining house "I've already told the other policewoman what I know."

"We understand that, and we are very grateful for your co-operation" Adam gave the old woman one of his nicest smiles "but if you could just go over it again with us that would be great and could help us enormously with our investigation."

"Blimey, he's a bit lardy da, aint he."

Stopping herself from smiling Kelly asked, "Can you just tell us again what you remember of that night."

The old woman walked into the sitting room and after waiting for the two detectives to follow she took a seat next to the fire "Well, I remember seeing Jorga come home from school, such a pretty little thing" glancing towards the window "about an hour later I saw that troll…" stopping herself she started again "I saw Mrs O'Brien leave the house."

"Did you see if she got into a car?"

"She walked, how on earth she manages to walk in those high shoes I just don't know." The woman seemed to be deep in thought.

Trying to bring the old lady back on track Kelly asked "Did you see which way she went? Was anyone waiting for her?" when no reply came Kelly pressed on "Mrs Murphy, what was the next thing that you noticed?"

Shaking her head slowly "Someone knocking on the door, these walls are so thin that you can't help but hear everything" Looking between the two officers "I know that everyone thinks that I'm just a nosey old bat, but you really can't help but hear things."

Adam walked across the room and sat down on the chair nearest to where Mrs Murphy was sitting "We don't think that at all" he smiled at her "In fact we believe that you are an asset to our case" leaning forward he patted the woman's hand "anything that you can remember will be vitally important to our investigation" hesitating he continued "now if you can just think back, you saw Jorga arrive and then Mrs O'Brien leave. After she had left was when you heard someone knock on their front door, is that right?" the woman nodded "Did you hear any conversation between the caller and Jorga?"

"Not all of it" she looked down at her hands "it was something to do with an accident and that Jorga should open the door. Looking back up at Adam "from the tone of the woman's voice she seemed to be getting a bit frustrated that she wouldn't immediately do as she was told."

Kelly's ears pricked up and leaning forward "Mrs Murphy, you said the woman, are you sure that it was a woman's voice that you heard." Looking over at Adam "I'm sure that you told our colleague that it was a man that you saw get out of the car."

"Oh, yes I did but after thinking about it the voice was definitely a woman" nodding at Adam "quite refined like this one!" looking down at her hands again "I think that I assumed it was a man because of the walk" she looked over at Kelly "you know sort of heavy steps rather than a woman's lighter step."

Exasperated Kelly tried hard to keep her voice level "you didn't think that it was important to call us and let us know that you had made a mistake. You do realise that we have lost time looking for a man!"

"Sorry"

"You told our colleague that you didn't get a good look at the person who knocked on the door, but that you did see a dark sports car, can you remember anything else about the car?"

"Again, I thought about that afterwards, I'm not sure that it was a sports car but more like one of those modern saloon type cars. Sorry, I don't know the types of cars" pursing her lips "yes, definitely more like a saloon, but I am sure that it was black. As for the man, no I couldn't really tell you what he looked like."

Swallowing down her angry Kelly "Can you tell me exactly where you were standing when you saw the person get out of the car."

The woman stood and walked across to the left of the window "Here" turning to look at Kelly who was standing behind her "you see I can see the street and their gate, but the front door is out of my view."

"Did you see Jorga and the man leave?"

"No, the local news started, and I wanted to see what the mayor was talking about" Mrs Murphy folded her arms "load of old rubbish as normal, but when I glanced out of the window again the car was gone."

Thanking the woman for her help and ensuring that if she remembers anything else that she will immediately call Adam, the two officers made their way out of the house and back to the car.

Kelly was still seething as they got into the car "Bloody hell!" hitting her hands on the steering wheel "Bloody sorry that I got the sex of the person and the car wrong and that you've wasted time on my nonsense information, sorry bloody sorry." Turning on the ignition Kelly looked at her colleague "The boss is not going to like this!"

Setting off down the road Adam shook his head "For a place with so many curtain twitchers I still can't believe that no-one else saw anything." Kelly agreed with him "I'll start looking through the CCTV again for a black saloon, it's going to be like looking for the proverbial needle in a haystack."

Arriving back at the station Kelly made her way directly to DCI Edwards office, where she found her superior officer sitting with her head in her hands studying the forensic report documents "Ma'am." Waiting for the other woman to look up

"We've just got back from Mrs Murphy's." Kelly walked across to the spare chair at the side of the desk "I'm afraid that you're not going to like what we've found out."

Elaine couldn't believe her ears as she listened quietly to what had transpired. Once Kelly had finished telling her she pushed back her chair and walked out into the outer office, clapping her hands to get everyone's attention "It appears that we have been looking for the wrong person" Looking at Kelly "Please explain!"

Kelly took a deep breath "DC Chambers and I have just been back to Mrs Murphy the nosey neighbour of Mrs O'Brien, it appears that she has remembered that the voice she heard was not a man but was actually a woman's voice." She waited whilst everyone settled down again, holding up her hands to bring the focus back to her "not only that but the car that she saw wasn't a sports car but a saloon."

DCI Edwards stepped forward "I know how you all feel, believe me I know" looking around at the angry faces "but we don't have time for anger, let's be honest we have wasted enough time none of which is our fault." Shrugging "We need to start looking at the CCTV again this time for the correct car and a woman driving. If you can all start again with your duties, and I will go and make DCS Collins day!"

19

The large black car turned off the main road and turned into the car park. The individual chose a parking space that had a perfect view of the children's playground and was close enough to watch the children, but not too close to raise any suspicion.

Taking in the scene the individual could see the mothers sitting around on benches that ran along the perimeter fence of the playground. The individual noted that none of the women appeared to be watching their children but were busy either on their mobile phones or chatting with friends.

The individual drummed their fingers on the steering wheel whilst watching the children as they clambered over climbing frames or played hide'n 'seek. That was all but one. She was sat on her own at the opposite side of the playground to where all of the mothers were seated, she looked so sad as she sat watching as the other children played around, totally ignoring her.

"There you are, my lovely" they murmured to themselves, "No mummy looking after you, oh, what a shame, maybe I can change that!"

Carefully getting out of their car and quietly shutting the door so as not to raise any suspicion from the assembled mothers, the individual made their way around the outside of the playground fence towards where the young girl was sitting.

A sudden shout stopped the individual in their tracks "Kylie, Kylie" a woman's voice could be heard calling from the distance.

At the sound of the woman's voice the young girl jumped up and started to run towards the woman "Mum, I thought you'd forgotten." The girl's excited voice floated through the air.

Without any of the niceties that would normally happen between mother and daughter, with a harsh tone and grabbing the young girls arm she hissed "Come on girl we have to get home now." Pulling the girl after her they hurried from the playground.

Cursing, the individual hastily made their way back to their car, staring in the direction that the mother and daughter had taken the individual muttered "Okay, so not today, but we will meet very soon." Laughing they turned on the engine and drove away.

20

Three weeks later, DCI Edwards stood in front of a packed meeting room "Right, quiet everyone let's get going" Elaine scanned the information that had been collated on the whiteboard "We all know what has happened within the investigation up until this point" stopping to look at everyone "what we need now is new avenues of enquiry." Taking a deep breath, she continued "Commander Fowler has now insisted that we carry out a reconstruction of the last time that both girls were seen. Peter Duffy, his press officer will be liaising with the media both local and national to cover these."

"Do we have girls that look like Maggie and Jorga Ma'am." Adam enquired.

Elaine sighed "I believe that they are going to use two young actresses."

"Ma'am, when are they planning on doing this, as the school holidays will be starting soon, and a lot of people will be going away from the area." Scott asked as he sat down on the edge of the table.

"Good point, but from what I have been told it will be over the next couple of days." Elaine paused to let this information sink in "Does anyone have any updates at all." When no-one answered "Right if you can all please concentrate on any leads that need following up. Once the reconstruction happens we need to be ready for calls both good and bad from the public." Pausing, "One other thing we will need someone to pose as Jack the school caretaker for the reconstruction" addressing one of the young PCs "PC Carter as you were there I would like you to do this, if you feel that you can."

"Yes, Ma'am, no problem" PC Carter blushed as he spoke.

"Thank you." With that she pointed at the four detectives sitting in the front row "Can you all please stay here for a moment, the rest of you can carry on. Thank you."

Once everyone else had left the room Edsel queried "What do you think that they will do for Maggie's re-enactment?" folding his arms "after all as far as we know she was taken from the school yard, where she was sitting waiting for her mum."

"It's always possible that the perpetrator may have been seen hanging around when parents were collecting their children" Elaine sat on the edge of the desk that was at the front of the room "But you're right we don't know if she was taken away in a car as we are assuming that Jorga was. We can only hope that seeing her sitting there might jog someone's memory."

"She must have been brought back by vehicle though surely" Kelly ventured "No-one would carry a child through the streets, even in the dead of night and not be spotted by someone." Looking down at her notes "Is it just me or does anyone else find it strange that in this day and age there are no CCTV cameras either at or near the school. Also, most 8–9-

year-olds seem to have a phone, but neither of these girls had one."

"We couldn't believe it when we started the house-to-house enquiries, not only no CCTV but not even one doorbell camera." Sott rubbed his chin "We're told that wherever you go these days you'll be on camera, it seems that it's everywhere other than Bournleigh!" the others all agreed.

"As both of the girls were found in nightdresses, where are their other clothes? We know that Maggie was still in her uniform. According to the report from SOCO they didn't find any school clothes in Jorga's room, so we can assume that she still had her uniform on!" Kelly ran her fingers through her hair as she spoke.

Scott immediately answered, "Every bin and alleyway was searched within a 2-mile radius, not only at the school but also both crime scenes. Nothing was found."

Pulling her hair up into a ponytail Kelly nodded "Whoever our murderer is they are obviously forensically aware." Pointing at the photographs on the whiteboard "If you look at where Jorga was found, how did they manage to carry her to the playhouse without leaving even one footprint? It was early morning, and the dew would still be on the ground but not one footprint!" looking directly at Elaine "How did they manage to get Jorga's body inside the playhouse without touching it or leaving even a shred of DNA?"

DCI Edwards folded her arms as she spoke "I know exactly what you mean, none of us can understand it. Dr Brown and his team were sure that they would find something.

A finger or shoe print a hair or even a thread from clothing that might have snagged on the old timber of the playhouse." Sighing "Dr Brown is as frustrated as we all are. There seems to be no rhyme or reason for either of the deaths."

"Ma'am, is there only one way in and out of the school yard?" Adam was flicking through the file that was balanced on his lap "I was sure that I read that there was a gate in the rear fence."

"Yes, there is." Scott opened his notebook "However forensics said that the gate was padlocked and that the padlock was so rusty that it looked as though it hadn't been opened for years. They didn't find any footprints or disturbance around the gate so that was ruled out as a point of entry."

"I would still like to know who holds a key." Adam frowned "do we know what is located on the other side of the school fence, especially around the area of the gate. There must be some sort of access, otherwise why would you put a gate there."

"Speak to sergeant Matthews, he was in charge of the search party. If for whatever reason no one searched that area then get him to send some PCs back immediately please." Elaine stretched out her legs "Right, with regard to the reconstructions me, Scott and Edsel will attend as we were there at the beginning. Kelly and Adam if you can take charge of the incident room and help to monitor any calls received. Let's all keep our fingers crossed that something positive comes out of this."

21

Two days later and the reconstructions had been set up. Elaine smiled as she watched Peter Duff, the press officer, flitting between the various national camera crews that had each marked out a place on the school playground to capture the drama of Maggie's disappearance.

Someone, who Elaine didn't recognise stepped in front of the camera's and holding a microphone started to narrate what was about to happen "The police are asking for the public's assistance in the murder of two little girls" turning to face where they had sat the girl playing Maggie "the first reconstruction is of Maggie Burnett, please think back to where you were and if you saw anything unusual on Friday 20 September" As he spoke PC Carter dressed in a long black coat walked across the playground towards where 'Maggie' was sitting "the time was approximately 5.00 pm when the school caretaker left the premises, leaving Maggie waiting for her mother to arrive. It is now known that Mrs Burnett did not collect her daughter on that day. This is the last known sighting of Maggie, until her body was discovered the following morning behind the shed, here in the school playground."

The camera crews immediately started to pack up and rush back to their trucks that were parked in the school car park and started to leave to travel to Hillview Terrace for the second reconstruction.

Looking at Edsel and Scott who were both stood next to her a shiver went down Elaines spine "I feel like someone has just walked over my grave." She stated, "right we'd better get going before we miss the action."

The road to Hillview Terrace had been closed off to the public, Elaine was amazed to see so many people standing on their doorsteps "Where were all of these" she nodded towards the opposite side of the road to Mrs O'Brien's when they were needed. Both Scott and Edsel shook their heads but remained silent.

The man with the microphone started to speak "This is the second reconstruction. This is the house of Mrs O'Brien and her daughter Jorga. On the night of Tuesday 24 September, Mrs O'Brien left the home to visit a friend" As they watched the door to Mrs O'Brien's house opened and a woman stepped out, dressed in a short dress, black leather jacket and impossibly high heels. Closing the door behind her she proceeded to totter down the path and across the road out of camera view.

The man continued "It is believed that a very short time later a dark-coloured saloon car….." as he spoke a car drove up the road and parked outside of the house. A woman in dark clothing got out of the car and walked up the path to the door. "A neighbour saw a heavily set individual, now believed to be a woman, exit the car and knock on Mrs O'Brien's door…." "This is the only information that the police have. There was no further sighting of Jorga until, unfortunately, her body was found a few miles away in a children's play area. If anyone has any information however small on either of these two murders you are urged to please contact the police immediately. Thank you."

Peter Duffy approached DCI Edwards "The TV Crews will be going to the playground to show the location of where Jorga's body was found, in the hope that this will hopefully jog someone's memory." Looking over towards the crowd that had gathered to watch "Isn't it normal for the murderer to revisit the site of their crime."

"It certainly happens on occasion." Elaine agreed.

Still looking at the crowd the press officer continued "So we could be being watched now by whoever did this." Elaine noticed the man shudder, composing himself "These reconstructions will be going out on both the national and local news starting with the 6.00 pm program, the papers will all have pictures of the girls along with writeups of the crimes." With that he walked back towards the journalists who were busy packing up.

Whilst Elaine had been talking to Peter, both Scott and Edsel had walked back to the car and were now patiently waiting for her to join them "Did he have anything important to say?" Edsel asked as he climbed into the rear seat of the car.

Ignoring the question Elaine ordered "We must make sure that both Mrs Burnett and Mrs O'Brien have FLO's with them before 6.00 pm when this will be shown on the news." Starting the engine, she put the car in gear and headed back towards the station.

22

The individual merged into the crowd that was watching the reconstructions, it gave them quite a thrill to see everyone commenting on what could have happened and how anyone could get away with two murders. No one took any notice of them standing amongst the locals. Everyone was far too intent on not missing any little detail of someone else's misfortune.

The individual, on seeing one of the camera crew swing their camera towards the crowd, ducked behind a very large man, after all it wouldn't do to have their face captured on film.

When they were satisfied that they'd seen enough they slowly, so as not to bring attention to themselves, walked back to their car. A happy smile played on their lips, and they whispered, "if this is the fuss that they make for two little girls let's see what they do for three."

Starting the engine, they laughed "So from now on the police will be looking for a dark saloon, time for a change I was getting fed up with this car anyway."

Driving away from the scene they started to sing to themselves, changing the words slightly "Pretty girlie walking down the street, pretty girlie who I'd like to meet" murmuring softly "no that should be who I'm going to meet."

23

At 6.00 pm the whole team including DCS Collins, gathered around the large tv screen that had been set up in the meeting room. The room fell silent as the news started: -

Good evening this is the 6.00 news with Brian James.

The camera panned to a serious looking man standing next to a screen where photographs of Maggie and Jorga were displayed.

"I am joined this evening by Police Commander Duncan Fowler" looking at the Police Commander "Thank you for joining me. Would you like to explain the circumstances that have brought you here tonight?"

Clearing his throat "Yes, thank you. We are asking for the public's help in tracking down the murderer of these two young girls…." Turning slightly to look at the screen "the young girl on the left is Maggie Burnett, we believe that she was taken from the school yard of Longmead Primary School sometime after 5.00 pm on 20 September by persons unknown. Her body was found on the school premises by the caretaker, early on 21 September. If anyone saw anything at all please contact my officers immediately…."

Brian James interrupted "How do you know that Maggie wasn't murdered there in the school yard? After all, if that was the last place that she was seen and also where her body was found, maybe she didn't leave the school premises!"

"Due to the nature of how she was found we strongly believe that she was taken to another location before being murdered." Duncan Fowler firmly stated and moved on quickly "With regard to Jorga O'Brien, the young girl on the right. Jorga was taken from her home after 5.30 pm on 24 September. A member of the public has reported seeing a black saloon type car parked outside of the home, with what we believe to be a woman driver. However, this is yet to be confirmed." Taking a breath, he continued "Unfortunately, Jorga's body was discovered early on the 25 September by dog walkers in a children's playground on the outskirts of Bournleigh. Did anyone visit that playground either later on 24th or early on 25th?"

"Do you believe that the murders were carried out by the same people?" Brian James questioned.

"At this time everything points to it being the same perpetrator, but we are not ruling anything out." Commander Fowler frowned as he answered.

Brian nodded and facing the camera announced "We are about to show reconstructions of the last time that both of these young girls were seen. This may be upsetting for some members of the public." With that the screen changed from pictures of the girls to show 'Maggie' sitting alone in the school playground and continued through both of the reconstructions. Once the film had finished the picture of the two girls was shown again.

Brian James pushed on "Are you looking for a sex offender and were these murders of a sexual nature?"

Before Police Commander Fowler answered he took a moment to consider how much information he should divulge "We have been informed by the pathologist that there appears to be no sexual contact with either of these murders. However, I am sure that both you Brian and your audience will appreciate there are certain details that I am not at liberty to disclose at the present time." Looking straight at the camera he added "I would ask everyone watching this program to think carefully about their movements on both the 20 and 24 of September. If anyone remembers anything at all, however small or insignificant they may think it is, it could be vital to our investigations." Turning back to face Brian James.

"That was Police Commander Duncan Fowler. I would like to reiterate what the Police Commander has said and would ask you all to pass on any information on these despicable crimes to the police. The incident room number is at the bottom of the screen, or you can phone Crime stoppers anonymously. Thank you."

As soon as the report had finished Elaine walked over to the tv and turned it off. Turning to the packed room "Right everyone, I would suggest that you grab a coffee and a quick nature break if you need one, before the phones go crazy." Just as she had stopped speaking the incident room phones started to ring "Here we go!" The room quickly emptied as the officers all raced back to their allocated desks.

"Keep me informed of any developments." DCS Collins spoke to Elaine as he walked out into the outer office and headed back towards the corridor leading to his own office.

Once it was only DCI Edwards and the 4 detectives left in the room, she spoke "We will need to start collating any leads that come in, shifting through the one's that need to be followed up and those from the crank calls." Elaine looked out through the open door to the outer office, where she could not only see but hear the chatter of the officers taking numerous calls. "Kelly if you, Scott and I set up in here ready to start shifting through any information received. This will allow us to send the necessary resources to follow up on any leads that need immediate attention. Edsel and Adam can you collect the leads and keep an eye on everyone out there." Nodding towards the outer office. Edsel and Adam both nodded and as they stood to leave she added "Would you ask Sergeant Matthews if I could see him please?"

As Kelly and Scott started to set up the room ready for what they hoped would be an influx of information, Elaine headed back to her office where she was joined by Sergeant Matthews.

"You wanted to see me, ma'am."

"Come in Ted" indicating that he should sit "Can you allocate at least two uniformed officers to follow up immediately on any leads either with one of the detectives or together, please."

"Of course, ma'am, but it will mean taking them away from the phones." Shrugging his shoulders "I'm afraid that I don't have anyone else, what with cutbacks and sickness, these…." he looked out into the other office "are all that we have."

"I have asked for further officers to be drafted in from outside of the area, but as yet Commander Fowler hasn't authorized my request."

Ted gave a half smile "Well what's new! Although maybe now that he has had to come out in public he may change his mind."

"I'm not holding my breath. If you or your team need anything please let me know." Stopping before adding "Bacon rolls and decent coffee wouldn't go a miss, I bet!"

"That would be much appreciated, ma'am." Ted called over his shoulder as he left the room.

Elaine lifted the receiver of her office phone and dialed a pre-set number, after a few rings the call was answered "DCI Edwards, what a pleasure to hear from you" Peter Duffy's Oxford educated voice drifted down the telephone line "How did you think that the reconstructions went?"

"Actually, Peter it's about the reconstructions that I'm phoning about." Elaine tried not to shudder at the sound of the man's voice, he really was a smooth idiot "Why haven't I received the footage of the reconstructions as requested?"

"Well, I'm sure that you are aware that I am a very busy man and I have to prioritize requests in order of importance." The man huffed.

"PRIORITIZE" Elaine couldn't stop herself from shouting "What in god's name is more important than the murder of two little girls!" Taking a deep breath and just about controlling her anger "I need the footage from every single camera crew and any journalist photos immediately."

"Now, young lady……." Peter stammered.

Cutting in before he could continue "Peter, let's get this crystal clear I don't care if the Queen herself has asked you for something my murders are your TOP PRIORITY. Do I make myself clear or do I need to instruct Commander Fowler that you are obstructing my investigation." Pausing for a second she quickly added "And one other thing Peter, don't you ever call me young lady again it is DCI Edwards. I want my request dealt with and I expect the footage and photographs on my desk by close of play."

When he answered he had lost some of the arrogance from his voice "I hope that you are not threatening me, DCI Edwards."

"Oh, Peter don't take it as a threat but as a promise. Good day." Elaine slammed the receiver down muttering to herself "Stupid bloody prat."

"Um, have I come at a bad time?" Elaine looked up to see Dr Brown standing in the open doorway of the office.

Leaning back in her chair she indicated for the man to sit opposite her "Honestly Chris, the man's a bloody idiot. He must think that other things are a priority for his time. What could possibly be more important than the murder of two little girls."

Dr Brown shook his head "Despite the best education that money can buy, unfortunately you can't buy good sense."

Elaine looked across the desk "You look tired Chris."

"If you don't mind me saying I've seen you looking better." He gave her one of his best smiles "Anyway the reason for my visit, I've heard back from the lab and unfortunately they can't find anything on the clothes or in the stomach contents that could point towards how Maggie and Jorga were murdered." Pinching the bridge of his nose "However, one of the scientists is a very keen seamstress and she noticed a strange pattern within the stitching on both of the nightdresses. She's sure that if we could provide the sewing machine that we think are linked to them, she would be able to positively identify if it's the machine that they were made on."

"Well, I suppose that's something. Chris have you ever come across anything like this before?" Elaine ran her fingers through her hair as she spoke "I mean, no marks, bruises or stab wounds, now if the lab can't find any poison how on earth were they murdered? One thing is for sure, they didn't die of natural causes."

"I've examined both girls in minute detail to try to find something but there's not even a small puncture wound on either of them." Dr Brown took off his glasses and rubbed his eyes "and now, as you say, if the lab can't find any poison where do we go from here. I have been in touch with an old associate of mine Professor Park, he is head of a lab down in Somerset." Putting his glasses back on "he's a brilliant man, his lab helps out a lot with cold cases, mainly at present cases from America" sighing "we just don't seem to have the resources to employ him. However, he is a great friend and I have asked him to look at my notes as a favour. He has lots of experience of strange and up to now unsolved cases, so fingers crossed that he may spot something that I have overlooked." Pushing himself up wearily from his seat "If I hear anything you'll be the first to know."

After thanking him, Elaine went back to sifting through the files on her desk.

24

The individual poured themselves a large malt whisky, raising the glass towards the tv "Here's to you Police Commander Fowler" sipping the golden liquid a smile crept across their face "Let's see how you react to three little girls."

An hour later the individual was sitting at their computer looking through the various car sale sites, which were full of SUV's and flashy motors "Something less conspicuous is called for" they muttered whilst typing in white ford vans for sale. After a few minutes a site loaded with various models, the individual sighed at the number of vehicles to go through "nothing too new, but nothing that looks ready for the scrap heap." Scrolling through the pages they suddenly stopped and reading out loud to themselves "White Ford van, good condition, only one owner, 2020 model, 45,000 miles, 2 ltr, diesel. Perfect." Jotting down the address and telephone number of the garage, ready to phone in the morning.

Stretching, to ease the cramp in their shoulders from hunching over the computer, they slowly stood up from the chair, as they did so they gave a small laugh "Let's look at you my beauties." As they walked across the room they stopped at the table next to the tv, to refill their glass before walking over to the desk in the corner of the room. Bending to pick up the photograph that had been taken of the school pupils a few weeks ago, they smiled again "Kylie, my beauty you may have escaped me once, but you won't get away next time." Placing the photograph back in its place on the desk "your sticky finger mother won't know what's hit her."

Laughing the individual raised the glass to their lips and swallowed the golden liquid in one gulp, savoring the feeling of the whisky travelling down their throat. Singing softly to themselves they made their way up the stairs to bed.

25

Two hours after the broadcast had aired the phones were still going crazy, nothing useful had come in and Elaine could tell that the team were beginning to get despondent. Elaine walked over to the door leading to the outside office, looking around she signaled to PC Carter that she wanted him.

Walking gingerly towards her, he asked "Is everything alright, ma'am?"

"I need you to do me a favour please." Digging out her purse and handing him £60.00 "Nip over to Jonnys café and get a round of bacon butties and coffee for everyone, will you?"

"Yes, ma'am."

As he turned to leave she added "If that's not enough tell them that DCI Edwards will pay the rest tomorrow morning." With that the young PC hurried across the open office and out of the door.

As Elaine walked back into the office, Edsel hurried across the outer room and entered the office just as Elaine was about to sit down. In his hand he held a sheath of papers "This is the first batch, Ma'am." He placed them on the desk and hurried back out of the door.

Picking them up Elaine divided the papers between the three of them. As they each started to read it soon became evident that most were of no help to the investigation.

Scott sighed heavily "This one…." He said indicating the paper in front of him "this one says, my dog is psychic, every time anyone mentions the young girls on the TV he walks to the window and growls" stifling a laugh when he saw a frown appear on DCI Edwards face "Sorry ma'am, but how can a growling dog be a lead?"

"I know Scott, when the reconstructions went out we all knew that we would get some…." Pausing to find the right words "let's say less than useful leads."

Kelly looked up and sniffed "I smell bacon sandwiches. Do you both want one?"

Adam appeared at the door as Kelly was about to leave "No time I'm afraid, we have just had what could be a very good lead phoned in." handing a piece of paper to DCI Edwards he continued to explain "A lady, Mrs Beverley Smith, living on Brockhurst Road has phoned in, she saw a black car with a woman and young blond girl coming out of Hillview Terrace. She believes that the car turned right onto the high street heading north out of town."

DCI Edwards jumped up from her seat "Right, Scott you come with me." Snatching up the paper from the desk she handed it to Scott "Kelly, sorry to leave you to sort through the rest." Pausing "Actually Adam can you send PC Carter in to help Kelly." Seeing the relief on the DS face she smiled "at least you can have your bacon sandwich!"

Both DCI Edwards and DS Baker grabbed their jackets and briskly walked out of the office.

Within half an hour they were pulling up outside the address of Mrs Smith "Well this is a step up from Hillview Terrace" Elaine looked at the elegant façade of the property and the well-kept front garden "Right let's see what she has to say." Elaine was surprised that as soon as they exited the car an elderly lady opened the front door and watched as they walked up the path towards her. Extending her warrant card for the woman to inspect she introduced herself "Mrs Smith, I am Detective Chief Inspector Edwards, and this is my colleague Detective Sergeant Baker."

Mrs Smith smiled "I've been expecting you, please come in." turning she walked down the hallway and into a very large sitting room "Can I offer you tea or coffee?" she asked as she indicated for them both to take a seat.

"No, thank you" Elaine said before giving Scott a chance to answer "Firstly we would like to thank you for phoning into the investigation hot line. I understand from the message that I have received that you saw a car with a woman and a young girl on the night of the abduction." Looking at the woman "is that correct?"

"I hope that you don't think that I'm a nosey old bat." she looked down at her hands that were playing with a handkerchief in her lap "I didn't know what to do, so I phoned my friend and asked her if I should bother you with what I saw." Raising her eyes to look at Elaine "she said to leave it alone, and that you would put me down as a crank." At this the woman looked as though she might burst into tears.

Speaking softly to the woman Elaine gently encouraged her to continue "Mrs Smith, this is a double murder enquiry, and we are pleased to receive any information that someone thinks may help us to solve or bring us closer to catching the murderer. So, no we do not think that you are a crank. Please tell us what you saw."

The relief on the woman's face was obvious to Elaine "Well, I had been to the little shop on the corner and just as I was about to cross the road this big black car came speeding out of Hillview Terrace." Putting her hand to her chest "I thought for a moment that it was going to hit me." Taking a deep breath "but I did manage to see a young blond girl in the front passenger seat, she looked terrified, and I think that she was crying, but I can't be sure of that."

"You said that it was a woman driving, can you confirm that?" Scott leaned forward as he spoke.

"Yes, it definitely was a woman" shaking her head slightly "although I didn't get a good look at her, only the little girl."

Scott pressed on "What time was this?"

Mrs Smith thought for a moment "Oh dear I'm not really sure, let me think.

I was going to have a sandwich for my tea, but when I checked the bread was stale, so I walked across to the shop." Putting a finger up to her mouth "I would say it must have been about 5.30 pm."

Again, Scott spoke "Did you happen to notice the number plate or part of it? You said that it was a large black car, did you recognize it? Do you think that it could belong to someone in the neighbourhood, or perhaps someone around here owns a car like it. Have you seen it parked around here before."

Mrs Smith looked stunned "I'm sorry but I really don't know." Looking past Scott and directly at Elaine "You see I don't drive, so most cars look the same to me. The thing that I do know is that it was a large black car. Other than that, I'm sorry but I really don't know."

Elaine opened the file that she had brought into the house and taking out a photograph passed it to Mrs Smith "Is this the girl that you saw?"

"Let me just get my glasses" Mrs Smith stood up and walked over to a sideboard that stood against the back wall of the sitting room, after finding her glasses she walked back and sat down "Now let me see" after studying the photograph for a minute "Yes, I'm almost certain that she was the one in the car. Oh, my goodness is this the young girl ………"

Before she could finish Elaine took that photograph from Mrs Smith's shaking hand and placed it back in the folder, speaking in a calm voice Elaine asked "Are you sure that you don't remember anything about the woman driver? Did you see, for example, her hair colour." Mrs Smith shook her head "What about clothing, could you tell if she was dressed in dark or light clothes?" again the woman shook her head.

"I'm so very sorry Detective Chief Inspector, I wish that I could remember but I was so shocked at the speed of the car and the look on the little girl's face that I really didn't take any notice of the driver."

"Well, as I've already said you have been most helpful" Elaine and Scott both stood "Detective Sergeant Baker will leave you his card, if you should remember anything else please feel free to contact him." Bending forward she shook the woman's hand "please, don't get up we can see ourselves out."

Scott quietly closed the front door and hurried to catch up with Elaine "What do you think? Why would someone tell her not to speak to us? It doesn't make any sense."

"We need to get someone to look through the CCTV footage again, specifically for the car speeding out of Brockhurst Road and into the high street." Elaine stopped before opening the door to the car "Damn it, I forgot to ask her who her friend is if you speak to her again remember to ask her, I'd like to have a word with this friend. Let's get back and see if any other useful information has come in."

26

The individual smiled to themselves as they replaced the telephone handset back on the cradle. Everything was falling into place. The salesman at the garage on the outskirts of Manchester was happy to hold the van for them, after he was offered the incentive that it would be a purely cash in hand purchase.

The following morning the individual caught the bus to the train station and purchased a ticket to Manchester. After finding a seat next to a window the individual settled down for the long journey. The next few hours were excruciating as they endured the monotonous sound of people's half conversations shouting into their mobile phone. Why do people have to shout on mobile phones they wondered to themselves?

After a few hours with the train drawing nearer and nearer to Manchester the individual started to feel the excitement inside them build. They almost shouted with joy when the driver's voice came over the loudspeaker announcing that the next stop was Manchester Piccadilly. As soon as the train had pulled into the station, the individual jumped up from their seat and grabbed their overnight bag and quickly got off the train and hurried towards the exit.

Once outside of the station the individual had no trouble in spotting the salesman, as he was standing next to the only small white van in the station car park. Once the pleasantries were out of the way and the money had been handed over and duly counted by the salesman who told the individual "Good to do business with you." The individual unlocked the van, carefully stowing the overnight bag on the passenger seat and drove out of the station car park towards the small hotel that had been booked for one night.

After a good night's sleep and a hearty breakfast, it was time to put the next part of the plan into action. Driving back down the motorway the individual thought about how to ensure that this time the plan would go smoothly. There was no room for error, and they concluded that the only way was not to rush it and that they needed to be patient.

At last, Bournliegh came into view. Turning off of the main road the individual headed for the out-of-town industrial site, where some months earlier they had hired a storage unit. They had been very fortunate when hiring this unit as the CCTV covering that area was broken and due to this they had been given a discount on the monthly rent, which was always paid in cash. The individual always parked outside of the site for a few minutes to try to gauge if anyone else was around, when they were sure that the coast was clear they would drive in, using a remote door opener that allowed them to enter their unit without the need to stop.

The individual let out a long breath once inside the unit with the door firmly closed and locked again, they always found this to be the most nerve-racking part of the journey. Stepping out of the van they walked over to the opposite side of the unit and pulling back the tarpaulin gazed at the big black car that had served them well for the first two murders

"Sorry old friend but you have to stay here for the time being." They muttered as they replaced the tarpaulin. Turning away from the covered car, they walked back towards another car that they had driven to the unit the day before, this was the vehicle that they used during their day-to-day life. Taking one last look around the unit, they drove out, only looking back to ensure that the unit door had fully closed.

27

Walking back into the investigation room, Elaine was met by Sergeant Matthews "I hope that you don't mind ma'am, but I took it upon myself to direct one of our marked cars to patrol the area around both Maggie and Jorga's homes, along with Brockhurst Road and the surrounding area."

"Okay, for what reason?" Elaine sat on the edge of a nearby desk.

Sergeant Matthews smiled "After I heard about the car being seen in Brockhurst Avenue, I had a hunch that it could belong to a resident. After all that's quite an affluent area and big black cars are, I'm told, in vogue at the moment." He shrugged as he spoke "I don't mean to be sexist, but a lot of the mothers in the Brockhurst area are very often in a hurry, my guys are always stopping them for speeding."

"Right, I'll ignore the sexist remark. What has that got to do with our investigation?" Elaine stood up as if to walk away.

"Ma'am, my officers spotted a car matching the one that Mrs Smith described." The Sergeant stood firm "I passed the information onto DC Jones, and he has gone out to the area with PC Cooper to talk to the owner." Pausing "I hope that's okay, you did say before you left that my officers should accompany any of the detectives on interviews or follow ups."

Sitting back down on the edge of the desk "Does it look hopeful Ted? Have you heard from Edsel?"

"Nothing as yet ma'am, but they only left about 10 minutes ago. I'm surprised that you didn't pass them on the road. I had better get back over to the phones, if that's alright with you ma'am."

After thanking Sergeant Matthews Elaine made her way into the office where Kelly had been joined by Scott "I take it you were informed about the car being spotted?" This was directed at Kelly.

"Yes Ma'am, I did try to call you, but your phone was engaged." Swallowing hard "I thought it was best to act on the information quickly in case it was the car that we are looking for. I was worried that they might see the uniformed officers and move the car."

"You did the right thing" frowning "I'm just frustrated that Scott and I were so close to where it's been spotted and didn't know." Sitting down at the desk "has anything else come in?"

DC Jones and PC Cooper drove along the high street before turning right into Brockhurst Road and then left into Brockhurst Avenue. Pulling in behind the marked police car which was parked at the side of the Brockhurst road. As Edsel brought the car to a halt a uniformed officer got out of the car and approached them. "The house is just down there, third house on the right." Looking into the car and seeing only one PC with Edsel "Would you like us to stick around, just in case."

"Good idea." Edsel unbuckled his seat belt and exited the car "Right, we'll go down first and see how the land lies.

Maybe you could park your car opposite the drive to show we have support."

Edsel and PC Cooper made their way down towards the house as indicated by the other officer. Edsel was aware that in an area like this there would be lots of CCTV and doorbell cameras, so best do everything exactly to the book.

As they approached the house he glanced at PC Cooper "Leave the talking to me, okay?" she nodded, and they proceeded up the path to the front door. Edsel pressed the doorbell and listened, after what seemed an eternity, footsteps could be heard in the hallway.

The door was pulled open, and a very angry looking man stood in front of them "We don't have cold callers in this area, and we certainly don't want any bloody Jehovah bloody witnesses, now get lost."

Edsel quickly held out his warrant card "I am Detective Constable Jones, and my colleague is Police Constable Cooper."

"And?" the man stood looking from one to the other "am I supposed to be impressed by that!"

"Not at all sir, but we need to speak to your wife or partner please." Edsel had spotted a younger woman standing in a doorway leading off the hallway. "It is very important that we speak to you." He directed this comment at the woman ignoring the glower on the man's face. "If you don't mind it would be better if we could talk inside" he glanced up and down the road "I'm sure that your neighbours will all have some sort of camera trained on us, so if you don't mind."

The man eventually stood to one side "Take them in the back room and don't be all day. Hannah will need feeding soon" With that he stormed past the two police officers.

"Please come this way." The woman spoke so quietly that Edsel nearly missed what she said.

After showing them into a room situated at the back of the house, Edsel again introduced them both "I didn't catch your name ma'am."

"Mrs Pamela Hurst" the woman whispered "I don't know why you want to talk to me, but if we can make this quick please. I don't want to upset my husband any further."

"Did you happen to see the TV appeal for witnesses in regard to the murder of the two young girls." Mrs Hurst nodded her head "As you will know both girls lived very close to here. We are talking to everyone that owns a similar car to the one, we suspect, was used in their abduction and subsequent death."

The woman's hands flew up to her face "Surely you can't think that I had anything to do with their murders."

"Your husband mentioned Hannah, is she your daughter? How old is she? Do you know if she knows either Maggie or Jorga?" Edsel was puzzled when the woman didn't answer.

Standing up Mrs Hurst turned away from the officers and took a photograph down from a nearby shelf "this is Hannah" pausing "Well this is how Hannah used to look."

PC Cooper took the photograph from the woman's hand "You said used to look. Can I ask what you mean."

Mrs Hurst looked close to tears "We had an accident. It wasn't my fault, but Derek, my husband, blames me." She wiped a tear away with her hand, that had run down her cheek "Hannah is now completely dependent on round the clock help."

"I'm so sorry to hear that. Do you mind telling us when this was?" Edsel followed his colleague in keeping his voice low.

"Oh, goodness" the woman sat down wearily on a nearby chair "it was just over 2 years ago. I take her to a rehabilitation center twice a week for physiotherapy, but it isn't doing any good and it upsets Hannah. My husband still insists that I take her even though I beg him to let me try something else with Hannah."

"Can you tell us where you were on Tuesday 24 September at approximately 5.30 pm please?"

The woman thought for a moment "Ah, yes I remember, Hannah had toothache and I'd managed to get her an emergency appointment with our family dentist, but I had to be there by 5.45 pm." Looking down at her hands that were lying limply on her lap "I had phoned Derek at work to let him know, but he insisted that I wait here until he got home." Lowering her voice further "he likes to see what I am wearing and that I haven't got too much makeup on." With eyes filled with tears she looked at PC Cooper "I know what you must be thinking, how weak is this woman to let a man dictate what she wears but please don't judge me until you have walked in my shoes." Looking down again "anyway, we waited for as long as we could but when he didn't arrive by 5.30 pm I made the decision to leave. I had to rush to get Hannah to the dentist on time, I couldn't let her go through another night in such pain."

"What time did you get back from the dentist?" PC Cooper looked up from the notebook that she was writing in.

"Oh, goodness let me think." The woman looked puzzled "I think that it was close to 7.00 pm. I was worried that Derek would be angry that his meal was going to be very late."

"Was he angry?" Edsel noticed a small frown appeared on the woman's face.

"But that's the strange thing, when I got home his car wasn't in the driveway. As I came into the hallway I noticed the answerphone light flashing, it was a message from Derek." Shaking her head slightly "it was very odd, he said that he had decided to stay at the flat in Crookside and not to expect him home for a few days."

Edsel exchanged a quick look with his colleague "Is that normal? Why does he have a flat in Crookside?"

Mrs Hurst looked up at the ceiling as if listening for any movement "His late mother left him the flat when she died. Sometimes Derek will stay there, if he has a lot of work on at the lab and it saves him the nearly 2-hour journey if he's late leaving work." She quickly continued "He is in charge of toxicology at the lab on the Bent Tree Estate."

"Oh, I see." Again, Edsel gives PC Cooper a quizzical glance. "Does he keep extra clothes there or does he normal take an overnight bag?"

"He has clothes there and a cleaner goes in once a week who does his laundry and makes sure that he always has a change of clean clothes and that his fridge is stocked up with essentials milk etc." looking down at her hands again "He doesn't like me going there, which is fine by me as I have enough to do with this place."

"One last thing if you don't mind, which of the cars on the driveway do you normally drive?" Edsel put his notebook away.

"Oh, I'm only allowed to drive the black one as it's quite old now, my husband only ever drives the grey car, he wouldn't be seen dead in the old black one." On hearing footsteps on the hall stairs, she hurriedly stood up "Is that all, I must see to Hannah."

Thanking her for her time the two officers made their way out of the house, and back to their car.

"Poor bloody cow" PC Cooper almost spat the words out "What I wouldn't give to have something to arrest that evil controlling bastard of a husband."

"Well, one thing is for sure we can strike that car off the list." Edsel turned on the ignition "but I know what you mean about the husband, I'd be more than happy to slap the cuffs on that one."

28

A few days after the TV appeal, Edsel was sitting at his desk when his phone rang "Good Morning DC Jones, how can I help you?

"DC Jones, I don't know if you remember me, it's Ms. Richards, I spoke to you recently with regard to Mrs Monroe."

"Yes of course, how are you?" Edsel pulled his notebook and pen towards him in anticipation of what she might, hopefully, have remembered.

"Well, I don't know if it is important or not and I hope that I am not wasting your time, but I felt that I should tell someone." She hesitated as if waiting for Edsel to answer.

"I'm sure that any information that you have will not be a waste of my time." Edsel lowered the tone of his voice to encourage her to continue.

"I believe that I told you at the time that I was sure that Mrs Monroe had told me that she was moving to Spain. "Well, after you left, I searched through my old files and sure enough I found the address that she had given to me saying that if I was ever over there to try to call in and see her." Taking a breath "As it was half term last week, I thought that she might have gone out to her villa and as I felt like getting some sunshine, I booked a short break to Spain."

Edsel tried to hide his frustration as he answered, "That's really very nice for you, I don't mean to be rude, but I can't see what this has to do with our investigation."

"Please let me explain, I decided to take a drive and eventually I found her villa on the outskirts of a lovely little old Spanish village. Just as I was about to get out of the car to go and knock on the door, he came walking around from the rear of the villa and started watering the plants……."

Edsel interrupted her "Who? You said he! I thought that Mrs Monroe was happily single after the divorce."

"But that's just it, it was Mr Monroe." Sighing she continued "She would never have invited him out to stay with her, she hated him."

Edsel rubbed his hand over his face and tried to compose himself "People change Ms. Richards, maybe since the divorce they have found that they can get on as friends…."

"You don't understand" She nearly shouted, "there is no way that she would be friends with him." Her voice cracked as she whispered "he used to beat her. She tried to hide it, but we all saw through the excuses of 'I walked into a door', there are only so many times you can have the sort of accident that leaves bruises." Giving a little cough she continued "He seemed really at home and not like he was just visiting. As I said he was watering and dead heading the flowers and brushing up the patio area, you know all the things that we do in our own home, but not something that you would necessarily expect a visitor to do."

"Well……." Edsel started to speak.

"No detective, please listen" she begged him "I didn't know what to do, so I drove back down into the village and found a little taverner." Laughing she added "I find that a strong cup of coffee often makes me think clearer. Anyway, I had only been sitting there for about half an hour when who should walk in but Mr Monroe. I wish that you could have seen his face when he saw me sitting there. It took him a minute to register who I was, you could almost see the cogs turning but as soon as he did, he went as white as a ghost." She took a deep breath "Once he had composed himself, he walked over to my table and in quite a matter-of-fact way asked what I was doing there. I thought what a bloody cheek, so I told him that I had come out to see if Mrs Monroe was at her villa. I thought for a moment that he was going to faint. He wanted to know how I knew where her villa was and how long I was going to be in the area. When I asked him if she was at the villa, he gave me a very funny look, not quite a smirk but like a grimace, it was very strange."

"Right, but I still don't really see what this has to do with me." Edsel was beginning to lose patience.

Ms. Richards swallowed hard "It just didn't seem right. He wouldn't give me any of her contact details and more or less told me to go away and mind my own business. Don't you think that's odd, when all I wanted to do was see an old friend."

"It definitely is strange, but from what you have said he seems to be a very strange individual." Edsel didn't want the woman to worry so offered "I'll tell you what I can do, would it make you feel any better if I contact Mrs Monroe to confirm that she is safe and well."

"Oh, that would be wonderful. Thank you, detective. I really would be most grateful."

"No problem, leave it with me and thank you for your call." Edsel ended the call and went back to his paperwork, without giving it another thought.

29

DCI Edwards along with DCS Collins stood in front of a packed meeting room. The atmosphere was very subdued as DCS Collins started to speak "Right, we need to pull everything together and see what we are missing." Looking around the room "Who has any updates that are not already on the board?"

Edsel stood up "Sir, PC Cooper and I followed up the lead from Mrs Smith" he indicated the note that had been written on the whiteboard "I believe that the car was driven by a Mrs Hurst, and the blond girl sighted in the passenger seat was actually her disabled daughter Hannah." Scott started to update the board as Edsel spoke "However, both PC Cooper and I have some reservations regarding the husband."

"Like what?" DCS Collins sat down on the edge of the nearest table.

"Well, there are several things that struck us both as unusual." Fixing his eyes on PC Cooper "You took a lot of the notes, can you explain please."

Blushing slightly as she stood she looked down at her open notebook "Sir, we first observed that Mr Hurst seems to be a very angry man and that Mrs Hurst is obviously afraid of him. Apparently some time ago Mrs Hurst and Hannah were in a car accident that left Hannah needing round-the-clock care. Mrs Hurst informed us that her husband blames her for the accident although she swears that she was the innocent party."

"Have you checked that out?" when neither of them answered DCI Collins sternly added "Then get it checked. Please continue."

"Mrs Hurst was expecting her husband home on the night of 24 September, but he stayed over in a flat that he owns in Crookside. She said that he would have normally told her the day before, but this time it was just a message on the answerphone when she returned after taking Hannah to the dentist. The message was that he was staying over at the flat and not to expect him home for a few days. She mentioned that she thought at the time that it was strange, but to be honest it seemed as though she was relieved that he wasn't coming home."

Edsel quickly added "Also she told us that he is head of toxicology at the Bent Tree lab."

"Really?" DCI Edwards asked, "Can you check that out with Dr Brown, as I don't know about you DCS Collins, but I've never come across a Mr or Dr Hurst."

"No, get that checked out asap." DCS Collins looked around the room again "Anyone else?" When no-one answered he continued "well we can rule out the lead from Mrs Smith and the car speeding out of Hillview Terrace. We need answers and I for one do not want to hear of another girl going missing." Standing up he looked at Elaine "Over to you, but we need to bring this investigation to a conclusion toot sweet." With that he walked out of the room.

As soon as the DCS was out of earshot everyone in the room suddenly seemed more relaxed "The DCS is right as we seem to be treading water and this really isn't good enough. We are getting a drumming from all of the news outlets, and I have been assured that if we don't get results soon Commander Fowler will have someone's guts for garters, namely mine!" rubbing her face with her hands "Edsel check if Dr Brown knows anything about Mr Hurst, if not maybe, discreetly check with the Bent Tree lab find out what you can about his movements on the 24th." Sighing she looked around for Sergeant Matthews "Ted, Sorry but I think that we will need to go door to door again around both Maggie and Jorga's home. I know that it can be a thankless task, but someone may have remembered something, we can only hope."

As everyone started to leave the room Edsel quietly asked if he could have a few minutes of DCI Edwards time in private. On entering Elaine's office Edsel quietly closed the door. "Right, what's with all the cloak and dagger stuff?" Elaine sat at her desk and watched as the younger man fidgeted in the chair opposite her "Come on Edsel spit it out for god's sake."

Hesitantly he started to speak "A few days ago I had a strange phone call from Ms Richards, do you remember you sent me to question her about Mrs Monroe." Elaine nodded "Well she told me that she had been out to Spain during the half term break and had managed to find Mrs Monroe's villa. However, she said that it wasn't Mrs Monroe that was there but Mr Monroe…."

"So!" Elaine frowned "Why shouldn't he be there?"

"That's exactly what I said, but she insisted that Mrs Monroe hated her ex-husband and she inferred that he used to beat her." Taking a breath "When I said that people can change she nearly bit my head off, insisting that Mrs Monroe would never have him to stay as she hated the man. She said that she later saw Mr Monroe in a taverner and he was none too pleased to see her there, more or less telling her to go away and mind her own business." Looking at his senior colleague "the strange thing that hit me just now in the meeting, was the fact that he wouldn't even give Ms. Richards any contact details for his ex-wife." He glanced down at the desk "the thing is that I told her that I would check on the welfare of her friend, but to be honest I completely forgot about the phone call until just now, what with everything else it wasn't top of my priority list. Sorry Ma'am."

"Okay, well I can see why you wouldn't have prioritized it, but maybe it might be an idea to ask a couple of the uniform officers to call round to Mrs Monroe's house. Get them to check with her if Mr Monroe had her permission to be at the villa and also confirm if she was also in Spain during the school holiday." Smiling at the worried face of the DC, "Now that's off your chest I think you owe me a decent coffee."

"Ma'am I've just spoken to Dr Brown, and he confirmed that he has heard of Dr Hurst, however he has not had any direct dealings with him." Edsel walked across to Elaine's desk and sat down on the chair opposite her "I have also contacted the lab where Dr Hurst works. After I explained who I was the lady on the reception was very helpful, she kindly checked the electronic swipe card data for Dr Hurst and confirmed that he left the building at 5.00 pm on September 24." Edsel hesitated "If he left at 5.00 pm that wouldn't have given him time to get back to Bournliegh and abduct Jorga." Opening his notebook "I did take the liberty of asking the receptionist if she could provide me with the address of the Crookside house, after some cajoling she did eventually give me the address.

"Good work, we need to check out that address ask Kelly to go with you." Elaine leant forward and placed her arms on the desk "If you go now you might catch his cleaner before she leaves for the day" Pinching the bridge of her nose ". If he left at 5.00 pm why didn't he come home that night? After all that's not late, he would still have been home by 7.00 pm. Something doesn't sound right."

As Edsel turned to leave the office he almost collided with PC Carter who was about to knock on the door. "Sorry sir" the young constable stuttered, he stood back and waited whilst Edsel left "Ma'am, is it a good time to give you an update on our visit to Mrs Monroe?"

"Yes of course, come in and sit down" she indicated the chair that Edsel had just vacated.

Sitting with his open notebook on his knee he started to speak "At first when PC Carter and I arrived at Mrs Monroe's house we weren't sure if anyone was at home. Just as we were about to leave PC Carter thought that she saw movement in one of the bedroom windows, so I knocked again and called through the letter box asking if anyone was inside to please come to the door. After a couple of minutes, the door was opened by Mrs Monroe who apologized for not coming to the door before but stated that she had been in the shower." Frowning he looked up from his notebook "the strange thing was that although she had a towel wrapped around her head, it was obvious that she was fully dressed under the dressing gown that she had on."

"Really!" Elaine pinched the bridge of her nose again hoping that a migraine was not imminent.

"We introduced ourselves and told her that her friend Ms Richards had asked us to do a welfare check." Pausing for a second "Instead of being pleased that someone had bothered she seemed really quite annoyed. I explained that Ms. Richards had tried to visit her at her villa in Spain and had become concerned when she saw that Mr Monroe was staying there." Shaking his head slightly he added "I asked if she could confirm if she was also staying at the villa during the half term break and this really did anger her, she stated very firmly that it was none of anyone's business who she invited to stay with her, and that Ms. Richards should mind her own business. I asked again if she was also in Spain at the time of Ms. Richards visit, reluctantly she said that she was not and that was why she had allowed her ex-husband to use the villa." Looking directly at DCI Edwards "the confusing thing is that Mrs Monroe had a light tan. When we left I asked PC Cooper if the tan was real or could it have been makeup, not really understanding women's cosmetics I couldn't tell the difference, however PC Cooper confirmed that it was in fact a real tan. It doesn't make any sense as the half term week was wet and cold here, so if she wasn't in Spain or somewhere hot how did she manage to get a tan?"

"I agree, leave this with me." As the young constable got up to leave Elaine added "Good work and pass that on to PC Cooper as well."

Three hours after leaving Bournliegh Police Station Edsel and Kelly pulled up outside the Crookside house of Dr Hurst. As they got out of the car Kelly whispered, "Well at least someone's at home, I've just seen a face in the top window." Edsel followed Kelly as they walked up the path leading to the front door. Ringing the doorbell, they both stood and waited, Kelly was just about to ring the bell again when the front door slowly opened, and a young man stood there glaring at them "Yes!" was all the man said.

"Good afternoon sir, I am Detective Sergeant Bell, and my colleague is Detective Constable Jones" both held out their warrant cards for the man to inspect "Is this the home of Dr Derek Hurst?" the man nodded "is he at home sir? We need to speak to him."

"No, he isn't" the young man snapped "If his bloody stupid little wife has sent you then you can bugger off."

Shaking her head Kelly queried "His wife, why would his wife send the police to his door?" when the man didn't answer she continued "maybe it's better if we continue this discussion inside."

Sighing heavily the young man stood to one side and ushered them into the open lounge area "Derek doesn't discuss anything to do with his family or his work with me, so I don't see why you need to speak to me."

"Before we discuss anything can you tell us who you are please?" Kelly glanced around the room, which she noted was exceptionally clean and tidy, silently she wished her flat looked as tidy as this.

"Well, not that I think it's any of your business but if it means you'll go away" the man huffily replied, "I am Jonathon Bridges."

"Do you live here sir?" Edsel had taken out his notebook and scribbled the man's name down.

"Of course, I bloody do" waving his hand around the room "you don't think that Derek does all of this! A man of his standing wouldn't stoop to cooking and cleaning."

"I'm sorry but we have to ask these questions." Kelly glanced at Edsel before adding "we were told that Dr Hurst had a cleaner who kept everything running smoothly here."

Jonathon gave a small high-pitched laugh "Is that what that stupid bitch calls me, I must remember to tell Derek that he owes me quite a lot in back wages." Crossing his arms "Now if you are quite satisfied that I am not a cleaner or a burglar can you please go, Derek will be home soon, and I need to run his bath so that the temperature is right for him when he gets in." With that he walked back over to the door.

Kelly stood her ground and didn't move towards the front door "There is one other thing that you can help us with, can you confirm that Dr Hurst was here with you on Tuesday 24 September please."

The man's shoulders slumped "24th, let me think" as he thought he chewed his lower lip "Oh, yes of course that was the day that his kid had to go to the dentist. Oh my god you would have thought that the world was coming to an end. That stupid bloody wife of his nearly blew up our answerphone with messages, I got so fed up with it that I nearly answered it myself and told her to get lost." Examining his fingernails "but I thought better of it. Derek would have gone nuts if I'd spoken to her and let's be honest I know which side my bread is buttered on, if you get my meaning." Walking back across the room towards the front door "now if you don't mind."

"So am I right in thinking that Mrs Hurst knows nothing about you and Dr Hurst." Edsel ignored the withering look that the other man gave him "How on earth does he manage to keep his two lives separate!"

"Okay, okay "Jonathon slumped down on the nearest chair "from what he's told me, and believe me its not much, he has always known that he was gay but in his earlier years it wasn't the done thing to 'come out' so he hid it." Pouting slightly "so when he met and married 'that woman' he tried his best to be a 'normal' husband and then of course the kid was born." Looking down at his clasped hands "We met three years ago. I was one of his students, it really was love at first sight, at least for me." Looking close to tears he continued "He was just about to leave her when the accident happened and that changed everything." Looking at the two officers "can you imagine the uproar if he had left her with a severely disabled child, he just couldn't see any way around it other than to keep our relationship quiet for the time being. When his mother died it was an ideal opportunity for us to move in here and gave Derek an excuse for his constant absence from their home." Standing he walked over and opened the front door "Now you have the full story so please leave, I don't want you here when Derek gets home."

As the two detectives walked past Jonathon to leave the house, Kelly stated "We will still need to speak to Dr Hurst, please get him to contact us as soon as possible. Thank you." At this Jonathon nodded his head in approval.

Once safely back in the car Edsel let out a long low whistle "Well, who would have guessed that." As Kelly started the car "I think to coin Jonathon's phrase, Dr Hurst likes his bread buttered on both sides." The two colleagues both laughed as they set off on their journey back to the station.

31

The out-of-town shopping mall was exceptionally busy as the individual pulled their car into a vacant parking spot. They smiled as they patiently watched as the passengers stepped down from the buses that brought people from the town out to the mall.

They knew from the observations that they had carried out over the last few weeks that tonight was a favourite of haunt of Jodi Smith, as the mall was always busy on pay day. She could, hopefully, carry out her business without being noticed by the security guards that patrolled the walkways and stores in the vast mall.

Just as the individual was about to give up, they noticed Jodi. She was hurrying away from the last bus to pull in with an enormous red shopping bag dangling from her hand. On spotting her the individual immediately got out and locked the van. Walking quickly, they tried to keep her in sight without being noticed.

Once inside the mall she made a beeline for 'Margots' an upmarket boutique. Feeling quite self-conscience the individual followed her inside. For a moment they thought that she must have slipped out of another door, but then they spotted her loitering amongst the very expensive lingerie. Watching from behind a row of coats the individual saw that with a slight of hand she dropped a silk negligee set into her shopping bag. Once she was sure that no-one had seen her, she started to head towards the exit. The individual quickened their pace and managed to get to the exit in plenty of time to whisper to the bored looking security guard, that was supposedly looking out for shoplifters, that he might want to stop the lady in the black leather coat with the big red shopping bag. With that they walked across to the opposite side of the walkway and waited.

Watching as the woman tried in vain to walk past the guard, only to be hauled back inside and marched towards the back of the store, where the manager's office was situated. Patiently they waited and after about half an hour the police had arrived. So that they didn't attract any unwanted attention, the individual took out their phone and pretended to make a call. Breathing a sigh of relief when after only another ten minutes, the individual saw the woman being escorted out of the store between two burly police officers.

The individual smiled; the plan was now in place. Hurrying out of the mall and towards the van they knew that the time was right to pluck the next little duckling away from their mother.

32

Just as Elaine was about to bite into her sandwich, which she had brought with her from home this morning, her desk telephone started to ring. "DCI Edwards, how….."

"Ma'am, it's Sergeant Taylor. I have a woman down here at reception going, to put it bluntly, nuts." The desk sergeant huffed "She's not making any sense, keeps saying if she hadn't been arrested her kid would be at home. She doesn't appear to be high. She says she will only speak to a detective, because the rest of us are to blame. Ma'am, I know that everyone up there is busy but if someone could come down and have a quick word please, I would be eternally grateful?"

Quickly looking out into the outer office, Elaine gestured to Edsel that she wanted him "No problem, I'll send DC Jones down. Can you put her in interview room 2 please."

"Ma'am" Edsel stood in the open office doorway "Everything alright?"

Elaine sat back in her chair and rubbed her eyes "Can you go down and speak to a woman who Sergeant Taylor has put in interview room 2. Apparently she is making some sort of fuss, and he can't really make head or tail of what the problem is."

"Not being funny Ma'am but isn't that something that a uniform officer could do." Shrugging his shoulders "I'm in the middle of going over the CCTV again."

Leaning forward and resting her elbows on the desk "She wants to speak to a detective and unfortunately for you, you were the first detective that I saw. Now the sooner you go and see her the sooner you can go back to the CCTV."

"Yes Ma'am." Turning on his heels he stalked across the office muttering to himself.

He stopped as he approached the interview room and took a deep breath trying to steady his breathing to a calmer level. Thinking to himself what a complete waste of his time when he had a lot of other things to do. Slowly he opened the door and was surprised to see a very disheveled woman pacing back and forth in the small interview room.

"About bloody time." The woman spat the words out "My kid is missing, and you lot keep me hanging about in here for hours."

Straightening up to his full height "Why don't you sit down." Pulling a chair out from under the table Edsel sat and placed his notebook on the table "Firstly, I am Detective Constable Jones, and you are?"

"Bloody hell, Jodi Smith." The woman slumped in the chair opposite Edsel.

"Right can you tell me exactly how I can help." Opening his notebook "The desk sergeant was unclear about the problem…..."

"PROBLEM" woman shouted, "Is that what the police call a missing child now a bloody problem."

"Sorry a missing child, I wasn't told that." Edsel softened his voice.

"If your lot hadn't nicked me last night I would have been home, and my Kylie wouldn't be missing."

Frowning Edsel asked "Can you start again please; you were arrested last night? Where were you arrested and for what?"

"Oh, for Christ's sake, at the Mall because someone said I was shoplifting, not my fault if something happened to fall in my bag." Scratching her neck "I've been holed up in the lock-up all bloody night."

"Didn't you tell them that you had a child at home." Edsel scribbled in his notebook.

"Yes I bloody did. Lot of good it did me." Crossing her legs "Stupid copper said they'd send someone round to get her. Last I heard they couldn't get anyone to open the door, so they left a note, telling her to get in touch with the police." Her eyes glazed over, and Edsel thought she was about to cry "She's only bloody eight!"

"Where exactly is home?" Edsel leant forward to try to calm the woman down.

"Hillview Terrace." The woman snapped.

As she said this the hairs on the back of Edsel's neck stood up "Hillview Terrace, did Kylie know Jorga O'Brien?"

The woman thought for a moment "Don't really know. They lived down the road from us, but I think that she might have been in the same class, but not sure. Why?"

Edsel ignored the question "When you got home she wasn't there, is that correct?" the woman nodded "Have you checked with her friends? Maybe when you didn't come home she went to one of them." He rushed on "Do you have family in the area that she may have gone to?" The woman just looked blankly at Edsel "What about her father?"

Shaking her head "Kylie is very much a loner; she doesn't really have any friends. We don't have any family locally and as for her bloody father he buggered off just after she was born, never to be heard of again." Stifling a yawn "I've been everywhere that she might have gone. I even asked the nosey old cow that lives across the road if she saw my Kylie last night, but no joy. The one time I want her to be nosey she takes a night off from looking out of the window, normally she sees everything."

"Right, when was the last time that you saw your daughter?" Edsel bit his lower lip.

"When she came home from school, I gave her some tea and told her to stay indoors and that I wouldn't be long." Putting her head to one side "I needed to go to the mall and Kylie hates going with me. I should have only been gone an hour, if it wasn't for your lot arresting me on false pretenses I would have been back before her bedtime."

"Okay, and you're sure that you have checked everywhere, no question." Edsel was starting to get very worried "Do you happen to have a picture of Kylie with you?" the woman took out her purse from her pocket and slipped a small photograph from the card slots, sliding it across the table. Edsel froze as he looked down at photograph, snatching it as he stood up "Please wait here, I need to speak to someone."

After quietly closing the interview room door "Oh no, for god's sake please don't let this be another one." He hurried along the corridor and after taking the steps two at a time up to the second floor he raced across the outside office and without stopping to knock hurried into DCI Edwards office.

"My god Edsel is the place on fire?" Elaine looked up startled as the younger man came hurtling into her office.

"Sorry Ma'am, but the woman her daughter is missing, they live at Hillview Terrace near Jorga's home" he rushed forward and handed over the photograph that Mrs Smith had given him "Kylie, is eight years old and as you can see blond." He stopped to catch his breath "Mrs Smith, the woman in the interview room was arrested last night for shoplifting......"

Before he could finish Elaine jumped up from her seat "With me" she rushed past Edsel out into the outside office, clapping her hands to get everyone's attention "We have another missing child, her name is Kylie Smith" hesitating she looked at Edsel to confirm the name "she is eight years old and could have been missing since last night. Adam get this photo circulated to everyone, Scott get Sergeant Matthews to contact his officers out on patrol to be on the lookout for her. Kelly go with Edsel, find out any further information that Mrs Smith can give you and then take her home. I'll contact forensics to meet you there and get PC Angie Case to act as Family Liaison Officer, it could be advantageous to have the same FLO as they both live so close to each other." Catching her breath, she mumbled "Firstly I'd better let DCS Collins know."

The next few hours flew by in a flurry of activity. DCS Collins had come storming into DCI Edwards Office. He had just endured a very difficult conversation with Commander Fowler, and he now sat looking very uncomfortable on the opposite side of the desk to Elaine. Clearing his throat before he started to speak "Elaine, I know how hard you have worked on these murders, but Commander Fowler is now insisting that we bring in someone else to oversee procedures." As Elaine was about to speak he held up his hand to stop her "please let me finish. DCI George Woods is being assigned to join the team; he will be bringing a vast amount of experience to the team as he was recently in charge of the murder that happened in Yorkshire last year."

"So, am I being taken off of this case sir?" Elaine felt tears prick her eyes.

"No not at all. DCI Woods will be working with you." Looking kindly at his DCI "You must understand that with two murders and now a third young girl missing everyone, including the Commander is under tremendous pressure. God only knows what the press and the public will make of us if this latest young girl is found dead. I think that for her sake and ours we must hope for the best and if that means swallowing our pride and welcoming help from outside of our normal team then we should grab it with both hands." Walking to the office door he turned towards where a now despondent looking Elaine sat "keep me informed and please be nice to DCI Woods." With that he marched across the outside office and disappeared through the door leading to the corridor to his office.

Slamming her fist down on the desk Elaine spat out "DCI Fucking Woods."

Looking up at the clock Elaine suddenly realised that it was 10.00 pm, stifling a yawn she stretched as she stood up from her desk. The outer office was almost empty with only Scott and Adam still working on their computers. Looking at their tired faces she stated "You two had better get off home, there's nothing else we can do tonight. Sergeant Matthew's team carry out a complete sweep of the town and surrounding areas and he has two of his officers visiting any friends and classmates that Mrs Smith has been able to provide names for. If I hear anything I'll let you know, but you'll be no good to me if you are both worn out." Heading towards the kitchen she stopped and turning around asked "Have either of you ever worked with a DCI George Woods?" both men shook their heads. "Okay, get off home now, but be back in early please." After the two detectives had left Elaine decided that she should also try to get some sleep, so after making sure that her desk phone was redirected to her mobile she wearily made her way home.

33

Early the next morning she was just catching up on the vast number of emails that had arrived overnight on her computer when her desk phone suddenly started to ring "DCI Edwards, how can I……."

Before she could finish Sergeant Matthews trembling voice cut in "Ma'am it's Sergeant Matthews. I think that we've found Kylie Smith." trying to keep his voice calm "We were asked to attend an incident near the railway station……" swallowing hard "and that's where we found her. Ma'am she looks exactly like the other two….."

DCI Edwards had already jumped to her feet and was struggling into her jacket as she listened to the details "We're on our way Ted." Frantically looking around the outer office to see who had already arrived "Have you called Dr Brown's team?" After the officer had confirmed that forensics were already on their way, Elaine hung up the phone and rushed out of her office. "Scott, with me. Edsel get hold of Kelly and Adam and meet us at the railway station." Seeing the confusion on the two detectives faces she added "There's been another murder." Without another word and with Scott hot on her heels she hurried out of the office and ran down the stairs to the car park.

Seeing DCI Edwards heading for the driver's side of the car Scott stated, "I think that it's better if I drive Ma'am."

Taking the keys from her hand "I expect that you'll want to phone DCS Collins."

With the blue lights and the siren blaring, it only took DCI Edwards and Scott ten minutes to get to the railway station. As soon as the car was parked the two officers quickly walked across to the taped off area at the side of the station buildings. After showing their warrant cards to the PC manning the area, they were immediately given both shoe coverings and gloves by the PC. Rounding the side of the building Elaine spotted Sergeant Matthews pacing back and forwards at the entrance to a disused railway siding. Walking up to him Elaine asked, "Where is she Ted?"

Turning slightly Sergeant Matthews pointed in the direction of what appeared to be a run-down shack a few yards along the railway siding. "Just over there ma'am" he wiped his brow with his hand "She's been placed in the exact same way as Maggie and Jorga." The man's voice cracked as he spoke.

Thanking him DCI Edwards and Scott made their way in the direction that the Sergeant had pointed, being mindful not to contaminate any possible evidence that the perpetrator could have left behind. This involved taking a slightly longer route than perhaps the perpetrator would have taken. As they approached the young PC who was guarding the body straightened up "the body is through there ma'am."

Carefully they made their way to a muddy path, stepping on the grass to the side of the path hoping that they were not contaminating any evidence. As they rounded a slight bend in the path, directly in front of them lay the little girl. Elaine gasped at the sight of her, she looked just like the others curled into a foetal position, dressed in a white nightdress with her thumb in her mouth and her blond hair plaited and laid across her shoulder. Both detectives stood silently looking at her, for what seemed like hours, neither wanted to leave her lying there alone in the damp grass.

Dr Brown's voice brought them both back to the reality of what they were seeing "I hope that you haven't walked any closer and trampled any evidence DCI Edwards, you know better than to approach a crime scene before I get here."

"I'm sorry Chris" Elaine apologized "I can assure you that we have been careful, and this is as far as we went." Dragging her eyes away from the young girl "I didn't think, I just needed to know if it was Kylie or some other poor little thing." Looking down at her feet and trying desperately to stop the tears that were pressing against her eyelids "We need to go and inform Kylies mother." Looking at Dr Brown "As soon as you know anything......"

"Of course. Now let me start. I'd like to get this young lady back to the morgue as soon as possible." As Elaine turned to go Dr Brown touched her arm "I'll get everything rushed through as quickly as possible." With that he knelt down next to the body and started to examine the area.

Within half an hour DCI Edwards and Scott pulled up outside Mrs Smith's home in Hillview Terrace, looking at her younger colleague Elaine muttered "This really is like de' ja' vue'" stepping out of the car she was aware of several curtains being twitched in the adjoining houses.

Taking a deep breath and with Scott at her side she made her way to the front door where PC Case was already waiting for them. After taking one look at the two officers' faces as they approached, PC Case raised her hand to her mouth and for a split second closed her eyes. "Oh no." was all the officer could manage, pulling herself together and swallowing "Mrs Smith is in the sitting room, ma'am."

On entering the room Elaine was surprised to see how tidy everything was, after visiting the last two children's homes she had expected to find this one equally as messy. Walking across to where the woman sat huddled in the corner of the sofa Elaine introduced herself "Mrs Smith, I am Detective Chief Inspector Edwards, and this is my colleague Detective Sergeant Baker." Indicating the sofa, she asked "May I sit down."

Suddenly the woman sprang to her feet "Have you found her? Where is she?" looking past Scott who was standing in the open doorway "Kylie, Kylie" the woman shouted as if expecting to see the young girl appear behind Scott. "Is she in hospital? Let me get my coat. Which hospital is she in?"

Gently taking hold of the distressed woman's arm, Elaine steered her back to the sofa. Once the woman was seated Elaine spoke softly "Officers were called to an incident at the Bournliegh Railway Station earlier today……."

"Kylie has never been on a train, what was she doing there?" the woman interrupted.

"Mrs Smith, a body of a young girl had been found by some railway workers….."

The woman started to shake and clutching for Elaine's hand her voice a mere whisper "Please, not my Kylie, not my Kylie." With tears running down her face, she frantically looked from Elaine to Scott and back again "No, not my Kylie."

"We are so sorry, but we believe that it is your daughter." Elaine watched as the woman seemed to age in front of her eyes "I'm sorry to have to ask you but we will need someone to formally identify her. Is there anyone that you would like us to contact to be with you." The woman just shook her head "PC Case will stay with you and if you would like her to accompany you she will." Looking past Scott to where PC Case was standing in the hallway "Angie, I will let you know when Kylie is ready for her mother." Gently taking her hand from the woman's grasp "We are truly sorry for your loss and rest assured we will do everything in our power to catch the person or persons responsible."

34

The journey back to the station was in silence, with both colleagues deep in their own thoughts. As they pulled up Elaine looked over at Scott and taking a deep breath "Who the hell is doing this?"

As the two walked into the outer office, they were surprised to find that the whole office was eerily silent. Elaine noticed the look on Edsel's face as he slowly nodded towards her office, following his gaze Elaine was surprised to see not only DCS Collins in her office but also another tall heavily built man, both seemed to be in deep conversation. Walking briskly Elaine arrived at her office door before either man noticed her arrival.

"Sir" Elaine stopped just inside the office door.

"Ahh, DCI Edwards nice of you to join us." Without getting up from his seat the DCS indicated the other man "this is DCI Woods. Whilst we have been waiting for you to arrive I have been filling George in on the two, now three murders."

"I'm so sorry that I wasn't here before, sir" Elaines voice dripped with sarcasm "but I felt that it was my duty to personally inform the mother that her daughter's body had been found."

Coughing to clear his throat "Oh I see, well now that you are here maybe you could fill us in on this morning's events." He glared at Elaine "I need to be in Commander Fowlers office in precisely one hour, so if you don't mind can we get on with it." Narrowing his eyes "but without the sarcasm!"

Pulling up a chair Elaine almost collapsed onto it as she talked both men through everything that occurred that morning, finally stating "Dr Brown will give me a full update as soon as he can, and I also need to hear that Mrs Smith has formally identified the body."

"Right" DCS Collins stood up "I'll leave you two to get all the information updated with the team and I expect to be kept fully informed of everything. Do I make myself clear." Both officers nodded their confirmation.

Once they were left alone the older man spoke "Well we haven't really got off to a good start, so I think that it would be better to start all over again. What do you say?"

Listening to the soft tone of the man's voice Elaine felt herself soften a little "That sounds like a good idea." Allowing a small smile "Why don't we grab a coffee before calling a team meeting? I don't know if I'm up to going over the details time and time again at the moment."

Half an hour later the meeting room was packed as Elaine walked in "Thank you everyone for being here, I know that a lot of you should have knocked off hours ago." Standing in front of the whiteboard "let me introduce DCI Woods, he has been asked to come and assist us. DCI Woods has a wealth of experience and was recently involved in the murders that took place in Yorkshire."

DCI Woods stood up "Please be assured that I am not here to take over the investigation but have been brought in strictly as a new set of eyes. I know that you have all been working all the hours that God sends, and I have no intention of taking any of the credit away from your team. If you feel that you have anything you would like me to look at, then please let both DCI Edwards and I know." With that he sat back down.

Thanking him, DCI Edwards addressed the room "As most of you will know this morning Sergeant Matthew's patrol officers were called to an incident at Bournliegh railway station, where unfortunately some railway workers were clearing brush, from the track side and came across the body of a young girl." Looking at the whiteboard where the photograph of Kylie Smith had been placed alongside both Maggie and Jorga. "We believe that it is the body of Kylie Smith, but we are waiting for her mother to formally identify her." Elaine turned back towards the room "Both DS Baker and I observed the body in its resting place, from our observation the body seems to have been posed in exactly the same way as Maggie and Jorga."

A hand shot up from one of the officers sitting near to the back of the room "Excuse me ma'am, but was there another note left?"

"I can't answer that at the moment, all I can say is that her thumb had been placed in her mouth with her other fingers curled onto her palm. As we know that the last two messages were placed within the curled fingers I would be very surprised if there isn't a note, but we need to wait for Dr Brown to confirm or deny that."

"Ma'am" another officer raised his hand and asked when Elaine indicated for him to continue "Doesn't it seem strange that all three girls come from single parent families?" a murmur went around the room "and that, as far as we know, all three mothers are ….." he stopped obviously searching for the right words "Well um, all three mothers are on the wrong side of the law. One having been arrested for being a drunk, one a sex worker and now the latest one being a known thief. It seems like someone is targeting a certain type of child or mother."

"A very good observation" Elaine didn't know the officers name "We need to do some research into who might have contact with all three girls or as you rightly say their mothers." Looking at the officer that had spoken "I would like you to liaise with DC Chambers to look into each of their backgrounds, such as school friends, are any of them on the child protection list, speak to any parole officers that may have dealt with the mothers." Pausing for a moment "I know that a lot of these people will have already been spoken to, but it will do no harm to speak to them again. Does anyone else have anything else to add." No one else spoke so Elaine closed the meeting "I'll let you all know as soon as we have any update from Dr Brown."

After hours of trawling through all of the information with George, Elaine stood up from her seat at the desk and stretched "In your opinion have we missed anything?"

George Woods shifted in his chair, he still felt uncomfortable about being brought into someone else's case "From what I've seen you've covered everything that I would have covered." He moved the pile of papers to one side and putting his hands behind his head "CCTV is very patchy around the estate where the girls lived, without anything concrete to go on like you I'm slightly at a loss."

Walking over to the window Elaine rested her forehead against the cool windowpane "Let's think through the three mother's movements again" turning to face the other DCI she sat down on the windowsill "Starting with Mrs Burnett, she was so drunk that she didn't even notice that Maggie hadn't come home from school. Then we have Mrs O'Brien who had a pre-planned meeting" at this Elaine made air quotes with her fingers "with the mayor on the night that Jorga went missing" moving to sit back in her chair "and now we have Mrs Smith who was arrested for shoplifting on the night that Kylie went missing."

"Listening to you list them, it sounds like these abductions were planned. Think about it Elaine" George repeated back to her what she had just said.

A sudden look of realization crossed Elaine's face "Oh my god, how stupid are we. Whoever is taking these girls has got to know the movements of the mothers." Snatching up the receiver of her desk phone "Scott, where are you?" Elaine listened to the reply "Great, go to the Mall and get a copy of their CCTV that covers the area around the Margots store on the night that Mrs Smith was arrested, also get any CCTV that Margots have around the time that Mrs Smith was in the store and then arrested." Listening again "thank you Scott. No wait, doesn't Mrs Smith catch the bus to the mall, try to get any coverage of her walking from the bus into the mall. I'll get someone here to contact the bus company, they normally have excellent cameras on the buses, we might be able to see if she was with someone or if someone was following her."

"Okay, so hopefully that might shed some light on Mrs Smith, now let's look at the others." DCI Woods pulled one of the files from the pile on the desk and after removing the sheets of paper he spread them out on the desk so that they could both study them. "Now Mrs O'Brien, who would have known about her liaison with the mayor." Taking a fresh piece of paper, he started to write "the staff at the hotel, if this was a regular thing which I believe you said it was then at least the receptionist would have expected them" scratching his head with his pencil "Who else? I take it the mayor wouldn't note this meeting in his diary, so we can assume that his secretary wouldn't have known."

"Well maybe not officially, but secretaries are cunning creatures, she might have overheard a telephone conversation or heard the mayor making a reservation." George agreed "I'll get someone to go over to the mayor's office and speak to her" adding "discreetly of course!"

"Good thinking. Right, who else? Did Mrs O'Brien take a cab to the hotel?" Elaine confirmed that the woman had taken a bus and a train "So not only is the mayor a womanizer but also a cheapskate." At this both detectives allowed themselves a small smile "Let's have a look at Mrs Burnett, from what you've told me it was not unusual for Mrs Burnett to forget to collect Maggie from school at the end of the day. So, anyone hanging around the school at home time and seeing Maggie sitting there alone, when everyone else was long gone, could be quite confident that the mother wouldn't show up."

"I'm still puzzled about the connection" Elaine frowned "Both Mrs Burnett and Mrs Smith wouldn't have any connection to the mayor and as they are all known for different, um, occupations where is the link!"

"Okay, I see your point" George tapped his pencil on the desk as he thought through the problem "Right, so if the link isn't with the mothers it has to be with the girls. What do we know about them?"

"They were all eight years old and blond. Both Maggie and Jorga had notes placed in their hand and their thumbs in their mouth, we don't know if Kylie had a note or not yet. All three dressed in what we think are homemade white nightdresses, of course I am assuming that Kylies nightdress is the same, but we need that to be confirmed. They all attended Longmead Primary School. Both Jorga and Kylie were in the same class, Maggie was in a different class, but we are unsure if they were friends."

"Why don't we start at the beginning" George stretched his back "I think that a visit to the school and another chat with their teachers and the head mistress would be in order, what do you think?"

"Let's do it, we've nothing to lose and you never know they might have remembered something that seems trivial to them but could be important. I'll let Edsel know and ask him to help Scott run through the CCTV that hopefully he would have got from the mall." Elaine walked out of the office to find Edsel.

Parents had already started arriving to collect their children, when the two detectives reached the school. "Christ" muttered Elaine looking at the pack of journalists that were staking out the entrance to the school "I see that the vultures are already circling." As they made their way through the pack, the questions came thick and fast "What are you doing about these murders?" "Have you arrested someone?" on and on went the shouts, ignoring them all Elaine and George quickly headed for the school entrance "Remind me to organize some uniformed officers to be here at the start and finish of the school day, would you please?"

On entering the building to their surprise Mrs Monroe was standing in the middle of the reception area glaring at them, without any pleasantries she stated, "Come with me, I don't think this is the right place to speak" looking out through the glass door "With that lot out there." Stamping away from them she hurried down the corridor and disappeared into her office.

As Elaine and George both hurried after her, George whispered "Reminds me of my school days being summoned to the heads office."

"This really isn't good enough Detective Chief Inspector" Mrs Monroe was now seated behind her desk "my school's reputation is being dragged through the mud and you don't seem to be making any headway at all."

Elaine couldn't believe her ears "Mrs Monroe you are aware that three young girls have now been murdered, perhaps instead of worrying about the reputation of your school you should be more concerned with the fact that three of your pupils are dead and the effect that that is having both on their respective families but also on their classmates."

Stepping forward and trying to calm the situation down George held out his hand to Mrs Monroe "I'm Detective Chief Inspector Woods ma'am" indicating the two vacant chairs "if you can spare us a few minutes it would be appreciated." He held the back of one of the chairs for Elaine to sit down and then sat down on the other "we would also like to speak to the girls form teachers, if that's possible."

Huffily the woman clicked a button on her desk phone "Mrs Hole can you see if Ms. Pearce and Mr Austin are still on site please, if they are can they come to my office immediately."

Elaine's ears had pricked up at the second name "Mr Austin is back at the school?" when this was confirmed "May I ask is his mother better now?"

"No, you may not ask." Mrs Monroe snapped "his private life has nothing to do with this."

Just as Elaine was about to argue the point Ms. Pearce entered the room, stopping as she recognised Elaine "You wanted to see me?"

"No, not me these detectives would like a word with you." Looking past her into the hallway "Where's Mr Austin?"

"I think that he's already left for the day, I saw him earlier hurrying towards the car park." Ms. Pearce looked at the two officers "I'm not sure what I can tell you that I haven't already stated to the other officers."

"Take them to the staff room, I have a lot of work to do." Mrs Monroe ordered, seeing the teacher hesitate "NOW, would be good."

"Certainly, sorry please come this way." The woman almost ran out of the office and hurried away back down the corridor, on reaching the staff room she seemed near to tears "I can't believe that this has happened again." Slumping down on the old sofa that was against one of the walls "three little girls" she took her handkerchief out of her cardigan sleeve and wiped her eyes "they were all such lovely little things; despite their home lives they were bright as buttons." Sobbing "Why would anyone want to hurt such lovely little girls."

Once Elaine was convinced that the teacher had no further information they thanked her and started to walk towards the exit door "Well at least most of the vultures have left for the night."

"Deadlines my dear, if you'll excuse the pun." George held the glass door open for Elaine "Not sure about you but I could eat a scabby dog and wash it down with horse piss, my throat and stomach both think that I have a death wish."

"Well, I'm not sure that I can provide a scabby dog or horse piss as you so elegantly put it, but there is a half decent pub just round the corner. I can't have you dying on your first day here." Elaine smiled at her colleague as they headed towards the high street.

Walking into the Red Lion Pub, Elaine noticed Jack Hill sitting in his normal place in the corner. He seemed to straighten up when he spotted the detective standing at the bar, Elaine just waved and asked the barman to take a pint over to Jack. After ordering their food and a drink each, Elaine led George across the bar in the opposite direction of where Jack was sitting.

"Anyone I should know?" George took a sip from his beer.

"Mr Hill the school caretaker, poor bugger found Maggie" seeing Jack looking at her from across the room she raised her glass in a salute as the barman delivered his pint, smiling he gave her a thumbs up in thanks.

"What do you think of that head teacher?" George stopped as the waitress approached with their food, thanking her he continued "seemed like she was angry to the point of exploding." Taking a fork full of his cottage pie "was she like that when you interviewed her before?"

"Let's be honest, we didn't get a chance to speak to her today before we were dismissed." Elaine swallowed a mouthful of cottage pie and grimaced "I think that maybe your scabby dog would have tasted better." Pushing the plate away "I know that this isn't going to be a pleasant thought, but we will need to go back to the school again to talk to her."

When George had cleared his plate, Elaine laughed as she asked, "How the hell could you eat that!"

"Listen my girl if you'd ever been hungry you'd understand." With that they both got up and made their way back to where they'd parked the car.

36

When Elaine arrived at the station early the following morning, she was surprised to see both Scott and Edsel's cars in the station car park. Hurrying up the stairs leading to the detective suite of offices she wondered why they were both in so early.

"Morning Ma'am" Scott called out from the kitchen area "you're just in time the kettles just boiled."

"What have I missed" she asked as she walked across the office to where Edsel was sitting.

"Couple of things happened late yesterday ma'am" Edsel swiveled his chair around to face the DCI "Firstly I have eventually heard back from the airlines with regard to any flight details for Mrs Monroe, one in particular has confirmed that she used to fly on a regular basis with them, but they have no record of her for the last 7 years." Looking down at his notebook that was on his desk "I also asked about Mr Monroe, and they confirmed that he has flown with them on a reasonable regular basis, normally flying from Bristol to Alicante."

Why didn't you call me, I could have come back" Elaine sat down next to Edsel as Scott handed her a cup of coffee. "You said a couple of things!"

"The CCTV from the mall came in late last night, so we decided that it was best to watch it with clear heads, that's why we came in early." Hesitating Edsel added "I hope that was okay ma'am."

"Sorry ma'am, we should have called you." Scott nodded "we've been in since 6.00 am and we think that we might have spotted something. Can you roll back to Mrs Smith getting off the bus please." Edsel did as he was asked "right, there she goes" Scott pointed to the woman as she hurried away from the bus "this man here seems to be very interested in her" the three watched as a young man also got off the bus and headed in the same direction that Mrs Smith had taken.

"What makes you suspicious of him?" Elaine kept her eyes on the screen.

"He seems to be looking around as if he wants to make sure that he's not being followed and then when we cut to the CCTV inside the mall he seems to stop and look in shop windows every time that Mrs Smith looks around." Edsel brought up the video from inside the mall "there do you see, she looked behind and he immediately pretends to look in the nearest window."

Elaine wasn't convinced "Maybe but keep looking. See if he follows her into Margots. I have a hunch that whoever reported her to the security guard is the person that we need to speak to next." Picking up her coffee cup "I'll leave you to it." Making her way over to her office, she wondered what today would bring.

At exactly 8.30 am DCI Woods strolled into the outer office announcing as he did "As the new boy I thought that the doughnuts would be on me." He gladly received a round of applause as the officers swooped on the bags of warm doughnuts.

As Elaine was thinking of joining them her desk phone started to ring "Ma'am its Sergeant Taylor, I have a lady on the phone that wishes to speak to you, not sure why it was redirected down here. Can I put her through to you ma'am?"

"Yes of course, do you know who it is." The sergeant apologized for not taking her name "Good Morning, Detective Chief Inspector Edwards, how can I help you?"

"Good morning, Detective Chief Inspector this is Mrs Hole the school secretary at Longmeads Primary. I hope that I'm not disturbing you so early in the morning."

"Not at all Mrs Hole, how can I help." Elaine's mouth was watering as she watched the officers in the outer office devouring the doughnuts.

"Well, I've just had a rather strange phone call." Mrs Hole spoke quietly into the phone "a woman rang asking if I could confirm that Mrs Monroe was indeed the head mistress at the school, when I said she was, the woman seemed very confused."

"In what way?" Elaine was having trouble hearing as the woman was speaking quietly.

"I'm not sure, she started rambling on about the photo in the morning paper, I haven't seen it so I was unsure what she meant. Anyway, I suggested that she speak directly to you if she had any concerns. She said that she couldn't do that but then, and this is the strange thing she asked me to give you her details for you to contact her." The woman hesitated "I have to go now, but I'll email the details to you." With that the phone line went dead.

Turning to her computer she scrolled to the news sites "Bloody hell" looking up she caught George's eye "come here" she mouthed at him.

Walking into the office he saluted "Yes ma'am."

"Look at this" turning the computer screen so that he could see it "how the hell did they get that photo." There on the front page of the local paper was a photo of Elaine, George and Mrs Monroe standing in the reception area of the school with the headline screaming: - POLICE AT A LOSS AS A THIRD MURDER CONFIRMED.

"Bloody hell that's all we need." George sat down heavily "any news from Dr Brown?"

"I was just about to read an email from him when I got the phone call that tipped me off about this." Elaine turned the computer screen back towards her and scrolled down to Dr Brown's email: -

Elaine

Mrs Jodi Smith accompanied by PC Case has confirmed that the body is Kylie Smith.

I have carried out a preliminary autopsy on Kylie Smith. I can confirm that everything looks very similar to both Maggie and Jorga's murders. I will let you know as soon as we have any results from the various labs.

We have carried out a rape kit test and this was negative.

There appears to be no immediate reason for Kylie's death, no stab marks and no sign of any bullet holes or ligature marks. Again, this death looks to be similar to both Maggie Burnett and Jorga O'Brien, this is just an opinion at the present time we will know more once the results from the various labs are received. I have asked them to kindly expedite this case as a matter of urgency.

Just like the other two girls she was holding a note in her left hand, and this simply read: -
Fingered Ligero which according to my trusty google translates to Light Fingered. On the reverse of the note was the same message as the others, Silencio del bebe del silencio, which we already know means Hush Baby Hush.

I am still waiting to hear from my friend Professor Parker. Now that we have a third suspected murder I will send him another urgent email today asking for his help. I truly believe that he may be the one person who can help us prove the method of death.

I will send the note over to you once forensics have finished with it.

Regards
Chris.

"What do you think of that?" George scratched his nose.

"Everything seems odd today." Elaine told George about Mrs Holes phone call; I want to speak to this mysterious woman to find out why the newspaper photo has upset her enough to want to speak to me." Looking back at the computer screen "Mrs Hole has just emailed me, wait a second whilst I have a look." Opening the email, she frowned "It looks as though it was Mrs Crispin who phoned. Would you mind holding the fort here, if I take Kelly with me." Seeing the slight frown on her colleague's face "I think that two DCI's turning up on her doorstep might be a bit too heavy, do you mind?"

"When you put it like that, what can I say." They both stood up and walked out into the outer office together.

37

Mrs Crispin lived 30 miles away in a small village on the outskirts of Claybank, Elaine had telephoned her before leaving the station to ensure that it was convenient for them to visit. As they pulled into the driveway of the house they noticed that a woman who they assumed must be Mrs Crispin was already standing at the open front door. Getting out of the car and walking towards the woman Elaine took out her warrant card for the woman to inspect before introducing herself and DS Bell.

"Good morning please come in." Mrs Crispin showed them into the sitting room, which was at the front of the house "please sit down, can I get you anything to drink."

"No thank you, we're fine." Elaine answered without giving Kelly time to speak "Can you tell us what seems to be the problem. In a telephone conversation this morning with Mrs Hole the school secretary of Longmead primary, she informed me that you were enquiring about the school's head mistress Mrs Monroe. Mrs Hole got the distinct impression that you seemed to be upset by the photograph in this morning's newspaper, is that correct?"

The older woman took a seat opposite the two detectives and after brushing invisible lint off of her skirt, she looked directly at DCI Edwards as she spoke "I wanted to be sure that the woman in the picture was actually Mrs Monroe as stated in the paper."

"Okay, but why?" Kelly leant forward as she spoke.

"Well, it's a long story but I will try to condense it as best as I can. We, my late husband and I, used to live next to Trevor and Betty Monroe in Herefordshire, before we moved here ten years ago. We were very good friends with them for a number of years. Betty was a teacher at our children's school, everyone loved her and wanted their children to be in her class." Pausing "So when I saw that photograph I couldn't believe my eyes."

"Mrs Crispin, are you telling me that a photograph of an old friend upset you to the extent that you now have two police detectives travelling 30 miles to see you!" Elaine tried very hard not to sound irritated "We are in the middle of a very complex murder case, and we really don't have the time to spend soothing people over a photo of an old friend." Elaine started to stand.

"I completely understand Chief Inspector, I'm not explaining myself very well. Its times like this that I wish Tom, my late husband was here, he would know how to explain it much better than me." Taking a deep breath "you see that's just it; it isn't a photograph of my good friend Betty Monroe. Please just give me a minute Chief Inspector." Standing, she quickly walked out of the room returning shortly afterwards with a photo album. After turning several pages, she handed the open book to Elaine and pointed to a woman in the picture "you see that's Betty!"

Elaine couldn't believe her eyes "Are you sure that the head mistress at Longmead Primary and your old friend are supposed to be the same woman?" passing the book over to

Kelly "people change over the years, maybe Betty has put on weight and that's what's confusing you."

"That's why I wanted to speak to the school secretary this morning. I'm sure that I don't have to tell you Chief Inspector that secretaries are a fountain of knowledge." She took the book back from Kelly "Mrs Hole confirmed that Betty is Mrs Monroe's first name and that she claims to have divorced her husband some years before moving to Bournliegh. I do understand that people can change and putting on weight can slightly alter someone's features, but I don't think that it can affect their height!" Seeing that both officers were looking confused "you see Betty was approximately 5 feet 8 inches, I'm not very good at the new-fangled measurements but I think that would make her about 178 cm tall" Kelly nodded her agreement at this. As Mrs Crispin turned the album around so that the detectives could once again see the photograph, she pointed to the man standing next to Betty, "that's Trevor, as you can see he's quite a bit shorter than Betty, which was always a bug bear for him, my Tom used to refer to it as 'little man syndrome'." Bending down she picked up a newspaper that had been placed under a small table at the side of her chair handing the paper to Elaine she asked, "Can you see a resemblance Chief Inspector?"

"Good lord" was all Elaine could utter.

On taking the paper from DCI Edwards Kelly's eyebrows nearly disappeared into her hairline "What the………."

Quickly interrupting her younger colleague Elaine stated "Mrs Crispin would it be alright if we take a picture of this." indicating the photograph in the woman's book.

"Take it please." As she answered Mrs Crispin slipped the photograph out of cardboard corners that held the picture in place.

"I need to insist that you do not discuss this matter with anyone until you hear from me again." As she stood she confirmed "It really is very important that you don't mention this to anyone." Pausing "and I do mean anyone!"

After the woman confirmed her understanding and she had been thanked for her time, the two detectives made their way back to their car and headed for the station.

Just as they pulled into the station car park they noticed DCI Woods and DS Baker exiting another car which was parked a few spaces away. Waving to attract their attention Elaine and Kelly both stood and waited for the men to join them "Where have you two been" Elaine looked at her watch "It's too early for the pub!"

George laughed as they all walked towards the station "We had a tip from the house-to-house enquiries that is taking place around the Smiths home." Holding the door open for the others "Why don't we all grab a coffee, and we can go over it with you."

Once they were all settled in Elaine's office with coffees in hand, George started to explain "It was just after you left to visit Mrs Crispin, I received a call from Sergeant Matthews that one of his officers had been speaking to a neighbour, a Mr

Ahmed who lives two doors away from Mrs Smith." Taking a gulp of coffee "Mr Ahmed tells the officer that on the night that Kylie went missing he noticed a white van driving slowly up and down the road. Thinking that it was a courier who was lost he didn't really take too much notice at first, but then about 10 minutes later he saw the van again, but this time he was sure that it was a man and a young girl in the van. He told the officer that he had a funny feeling that things weren't right." As Elaine was about to speak he held up his hand to stop her and smiling added "Because of his 'feeling' he made a note of the registration number. Thank God for curtain twitchers."

"OMG, really!" Elaine lent forward "Please tell me that we can trace the owner."

"We have a name and an address." As Elaine started to stand George continued "Hold on, hold on" indicating for his colleague to take a seat "Not sure about the name but the address doesn't exist." Seeing confusion on Kelly's face "well in theory it exists but not as a dwelling it's a postal delivery service, you know you hire a post box so that you can collect packages, letters etc. at your leisure."

"The name, what's the name." Elaine couldn't hid her frustration.

"Alejo Ruiz." Scott stated.

"Alejo Ruiz?" Elaine repeated the name as if she couldn't believe it "Is that Spanish?"

"Si Senora" George bowed his head as he spoke "apparently according to a very nice lady a Helen Downs at the postal place said that Senor Ruiz never comes for his post himself, she told us it's normally an older gentleman that collects everything for him. In fact, she doesn't think that she has ever seen him." Looking down into his now empty coffee cup "but they do have a very old CCTV system, she couldn't download it herself, so she is contacting the manager to do this for us and will let us know as soon as its available."

"Now that we have a sighting of the white van and number plate, can you two arrange to look at the ANPR for the night of Kylies abduction and try to see where that van goes." As Kelly and Scott stood to leave "I know that we've done it before, but can you also look through the CCTV in the area, now that we have something to focus on it may give us some answers."

"How did you get on with Mrs Crispin?" George settled back in his chair as Elaine went through everything that the woman had told them. "I don't suppose, by any chance that Mr Monroe is Spanish?"

Elaine shook her head "No, I'm afraid not!"

"No, but he is an older man!" Elaine stretched as she stood up from her chair "I think that we had better go and update DCS Collins."

38

The individual smiled as they re-read the morning newspaper "So at last something is making them take notice." They laughed as they spoke "If this is the attention I get with three I wonder what they will do when there's four or maybe five."

Knowing that the wonderful Dr Brown was supposed to be the best pathologist in the south of England, the individual was amazed that the method that had been used to kill the girls hadn't been discovered, it was totally unbelievable.

The individual walked over to the desk in the corner of the sitting room, opening a draw they took out a map of the local area. "Right" they said to themselves "Now let's see where I have already used" taking a red pen from a pen holder on the top of the desk they walked over to the dining table and spread the map out. Taking the top off the pen they circled Longmead primary school, the children's playground in the woods and finally drew a circle at the side of the railway siding just south of the railway station.

They stood studying the map and eventually drew a circle around a location that they decided would be the perfect resting place for their next victim. Smiling to themselves they muttered "If the police won't come to me, perhaps it's time that I gave them a helping hand and left them a present on their own doorstep." Scratching their head with the end of the pen "I'm going to have to be very careful with my timings and *ensure that they have something to keep them occupied away from the police station,"*

Whistling softly, they made their way out of the bouse to complete their normal everyday chores.

DCS Collins walked into the meeting room where the detectives were waiting for him, making his way to the front of the room he stood and looked at the information displayed on the whiteboards "Right, let's get started."

Elaine stood up and moved to the side of the whiteboard "As we all know we now have three young girls who have been murdered." Pointing to each one individually "There are several coincidences between the three. The first is that all of them are from troubled single parent families, the second that none of the fathers have anything to do with them, thirdly they all attend the same school and finally it appears that the perpetrator must know the girls or their mothers. This would be the only way that this person would know when the girls were likely to be on their own."

"That's all very well, but nothing that you have just said is new to any of us." DCS Collins crossed his arms as he spoke.

"I think that it's important that we recap everything as it will focus our minds, if you don't mind Sir?" once the DCS nodded his approval Elaine continued "All the girls were dressed in white nightdresses which we believe are homemade, and all had a note left with them, which was handwritten in Spanish. Dr Brown has been unable, at this point, to determine a reason for their deaths. He is hoping that Professor Parker, who specializes in unusual deaths, will be able to help, as yet he has not heard back from him."

"We need him on board now, get Dr Brown to send his details through to me." Frowning DCS Collins stated, "I'll pass the details to the Commander, I'm sure he can pull some strings to get him onboard."

"At present Kelly and Scott are chasing up a lead on a white van that was seen in the vicinity of Kylie's home, the owner is Alejo Ruiz, but we have no residential address." Elaine looked at Scott "can you give us an update on how things are going."

Coughing to clear his throat "We have found the van on ANPR travelling down Hillview Terrace and entering the High Street, unfortunately we do not, as yet, have a clear view of the driver although we believe that there might also be a passenger but that is also unclear." Opening his notebook "from the High Street the van appears to travel West out of the town but is lost due to there being no CCTV once you are a mile or so from the edge of Bournliegh." Indicating Kelly "we are going to continue looking and hope that the van is driven back through the town later in the evening."

"Edsel, any new information on the man that you spotted following Jodi Smith into the mall?" Elaine sat on the edge of the nearby desk.

"I sent out the picture of him to the officers who patrol the area around the mall and one of them recognised him as a petty thief, apparently he steals to feed his drug habit so I believe that he can be ruled out as a suspect in the murders." As Elaine was about to speak Edsel asked "If I may ma'am, I have again spoken to the airlines and the ferry companies none of them have any record of Mrs Monroe travelling with them over the last 7 or so years" taking a breath "however, they do have records of both Mr Monroe and Mr Ruiz flying with them. Both men flew from Bristol to Alicante and back on several occasions, but never together and never during the same time period. I have also spoken to the passport office over in Cardiff who have confirmed that no passport has ever been issued to a Mr Alejo Ruiz, which in itself isn't surprising if he is a Spanish citizen."

"Leave that with me." DCS Collins straightened up in his seat "I'll see if we can get someone in the foreign office to speak to the Spanish Consulate to check if Mr Ruiz has a passport and hopefully we can get a copy with a photograph."

"Have you checked with the DVLA?" Elaine started to update the board as she spoke.

"Yes ma'am, no driving license has ever been issued for him. But again, if he is a Spanish national he could still be using his Spanish driving license, I believe it would be valid for 6 months if he is permanently resident here." Edsel looked for confirmation from Scott who nodded his agreement.

"Now the next strange thing to cover off is the visit to Mrs Crispin." Tapping the photograph that was pinned on the board alongside a copy of the mornings newspaper, Elaine continued "Mrs Crispin is convinced that the woman pictured in the newspaper is not Mrs Betty Monroe." With a small smile "she is convinced that this woman must be an imposter, as she looks shorter and rounder than the woman that she used to be friends with."

"Oh, for god's sake" the outburst was from DCS Collins "Doesn't she realise that we all get rounder as we get older and how can you tell the height of someone from that photograph. I think we sideline that information along with psychic dogs!" sighing he stood up "so really we are no further on than we were at the start. Commander Fowler is on the warpath already, I'm not sure how he is going to take the news that we still have no idea, and no firm leads. We need to catch this bastard before he or she strikes again."

Just as they were about to wrap up the meeting the door to the room opened, and a smiling Dr Brown entered "Sorry to interrupt but I think that you will want to hear this." seeing the DCS in the room "Oh, hi John I didn't realise that you'd also be here, so you've saved my poor old legs the effort of climbing up another two sets of stairs to your office."

"I'm glad to be of assistance." DCS Collins smiled as he sat back down "now what do you have for us."

"I've just had a very pleasant conversation with Professor Parker, after explaining about the murders and the fact that I cannot find any obvious reason for their deaths, he has kindly agreed to re-examine them." Acknowledging DCS Collins "I hope that your budget will accommodate."

"I'm sure Commander Fowler would pay a king's ransom at the moment if we can solve these crimes. When are you expecting him?"

"That's good to hear, as he's arriving tomorrow morning. He wants to see all of the results from the other labs as well, so I need to get back to ensure that everything is ready for him when he arrives tomorrow" with that Dr Brown hurried out of the room.

The detectives all sat silently for a moment, eventually DCS Collins broke the silence "Right, I'm going to leave you to it. Let me know as soon as the good Professor comes to any conclusion." With that he followed the doctor and left the room.

"If I was a praying woman I would now be down on my knees, however as I'm not I'll do the next best thing and keep my fingers tightly crossed." Elaine looked at the other detectives "Right come on back to work."

40

Elaine looked deep in thought as George walked into her office "Penny for them." He placed a take-out cup of coffee in front of her "I'm told that you like Latte with a double shot is that right?"

"You know the way to a woman's thoughts." Elaine laughed as she picked up the coffee and took a sip "I was just thinking, you remember the day that we went to the school and spoke to Ms. Pearce" George nodded "Well it didn't occur to me at the time that Mrs Monroe didn't seem to want to talk to us, she managed to get us out of her office very quickly and due to how upset Ms. Pearce was it slipped my mind that we should have gone back and talk to her."

"Okay, but is there any reason for us needing to?" George leaned back in his chair and studied Elaine's face "Something is bothering you, what is it?"

"I'm not sure, but something doesn't feel right." Running her fingers through her hair "Think about this, if you were a head teacher at a school where three of your pupils had been murdered wouldn't you be jumping up and down and wanting to know exactly what the police were doing to catch the killer." Frowning "I bloody well know I would."

"You know you have a very good point. She hasn't really seemed that concerned at all." Scratching his ear "As it's Sunday I think that we pay Mrs Monroe a surprise visit at home, what do you say. Let's see how she reacts with two DCI's beating on her door."

After letting the rest of the team know where they were going the two set off to visit the woman at home.

Mrs Monroe's home was set in a small cul-de-sac of detached houses on the edge of Bournliegh. After deciding that they didn't want to arouse any suspicion from nosey neighbours they parked the car at the end of the adjoining street. Discreetly looking around as they walked into the cul-de-sac neither detective could see any sign of being watched. They quickly walked up the front path of Mrs Monroe's home, it took several minutes for the door to be opened and the shock on the woman's face at seeing the two detectives standing there was a look of combined shock and outrage.

Her voice shaking "How dare you come to my home unannounced." Breathing heavily "and on a Sunday."

George stepped forward "We wouldn't disturb you if it wasn't important." Elaine noticed that he was using an authoritative tone which would normally be used in an interview situation "now, we can either speak to you here or you can come down to the station." When the woman didn't answer he turned slightly to Elaine "Would you mind calling for a patrol car to come and take Mrs Monroe to the station."

As Elaine pulled out her mobile the woman stepped back into the hall and opened the door fully "There's no need for that, I would prefer to speak here." Glancing over George's shoulder, Mrs Monroe quickly looked up and down the road before continuing "The neighbours will have enough to gossip about without me being carted off in a police car. Please come in." Showing them into a bright front room and indicating for them both to sit down on the sofa as she sat in the armchair facing them. "I'm sorry if I was short with you, but you must understand that it's not every day that two officers turn up, without notice, on my front doorstep." When neither detective responded, "What is so important that it couldn't wait until tomorrow."

"Well, can you tell us about your ex-husband? Do you know where he is living? And how we can contact him?" As George spoke Elaine took out a notepad.

"I can't for the life of me think what my ex-husband has to do with you DCI Woods." The woman's voice still held a slight tremble.

"For one thing, we have been given information that he is a regular visitor to your villa in Spain.........." Noticing the woman suddenly lost the colour from her face George pressed on "Also we would like to know any information that you have on a Mr Ruiz."

Fiddling with her skirt the woman seemed to be trying to compose herself "I still don't understand why anything to do with my ex-husband is any of yours or anyone else's business. I can allow anyone that I want to visit my villa, there is, as far as I'm aware no law against it."

Elaine leant forward "When was the last time that you went to the villa?"

"Oh goodness" the woman seemed to be caught off guard by the question "Um, I don't really know." Putting her hand to her mouth as if thinking "I normally try to fly out at least twice a year. Now that we are out of the EU it makes it more difficult."

"Oh right, so when was the last time!" Elaine tried not to show her confusion.

"I think that it was around Christmas of last year. As you know I have to go during school holidays." Interlacing her fingers "I really don't see………"

Interrupting the woman Elaine continued "Do you ever go out to the villa when your ex-husband is there?" the woman shook her head "so if you don't want to be there at the same time how do you contact him? And how does he get the keys for the villa?, I take it he doesn't have his own set."

"Look really I don't know what this is all about, does it really matter how I contact him or if he has a set of keys." The woman was starting to get agitated, sighing "I have a lady in the village that looks after the villa when I'm not there. She has permission to let my ex-husband have the key."

"Right, we will need her name and contact details." Elaine sat poised to write down the information "So that covers your ex-husband but what about Mr Ruiz, how do you know him?"

The woman stiffened "I don't! I never said that I knew him, I have no idea who he is." Slumping in her chair slightly "maybe he's a friend of Trevor's…" stopping herself "I mean my ex-husband, but I don't know him. I really do need to get on, if there's nothing else."

"Nearly done, but before we finish could I possibly use your bathroom please." George wriggled in his seat "Too much coffee this morning!"

Giving a heavy sigh "I suppose so, if you really need to." She frowned at George "top of the stairs first on the left."

Whilst waiting for her colleague to join her Elaine thanked Mrs Monroe for her time and reminded her that should she think of anything else to please contact the station immediately.

41

After parking the car at the station, they immediately made their way up to the investigation office. Looking around Elaine was pleased to note that the other four detectives were all working at their desks.

"While you get the others together, I just want to phone a couple of people and also try and grab a quick word with Dr Brown. Can you give me an hour or so." Walking away from his colleague George added "all will be explained."

As they waited for George to join them, Elaine impatiently paced back and forth "Ma'am, could you stop please, you're making me dizzy." Kelly smiled as she spoke.

"Sorry, sorry I was just trying to piece everything together….." stopping as the meeting room door opened and DCS Collins followed closely by George entered the room. "Sir."

"Good afternoon all. This had better be good" DCS Collins sat down "I was about to tuck into a lovely roast dinner."

George walked to the front of the room "Sir, I believe that DCI Edwards and I have made some very important strides within the investigation this morning." He started to explain "We visited Mrs Monroe at home this morning and to say that she was none too pleased was an understatement. She has told us that she flew out to Spain over the last Christmas holiday, which from the excellent information that DC Jones was given is not possible as none of the airlines have her down as a passenger." He perched on the edge of the nearest table "I have managed to speak to the lady that looks after Mrs Monroe's villa, she confirmed that she has not seen Mrs Monroe for a number of years and that it is always Mr Monroe who stays at the villa or at least who always collects the key from her. She told me that she has made several enquiries, asking when she will see Mrs Monroe and if she is well, but each time he manages to avoid answering the question, so eventually she gave up asking." Scratching his neck, he continued "I just had a feeling that I needed to look around, so I made an excuse that I needed to use the bathroom. Luckily for me one of the bedroom doors was slightly open and there in all its glory was a sewing machine….."

"Sorry, but do you know how many ladies have a sewing machine, even my mum has one." Seeing the look on DCI Woods face, Edsel fell quiet.

"If I may continue Detective Constable! Do all ladies including your mother have this?" taking a small evidence bag from his trousers pocket he held it up for the others to see "I may not be an expert, but this looks suspiciously like linen to me."

"Oh my god, how did you manage that." Elaine was shocked "but more importantly has it been compromised?

"Not at all, that's the beauty of always making sure that you are fully equipped before going out on a job." George took out several empty evidence bags from his pocket "I haven't laid a finger on it."

"Well done, can we get that straight over to the lab asap." DCS Collins tapped his lip as he thought "Unfortunately due to the fact that you didn't have a search warrant it can't be used in court." The DCS went to stand up.

"That's not all, Sir." George quickly spoke to stop the senior officer leaving "On reading through the files when I first came on board I was sure that when the first child, Maggie, was found that Dr Brown had mentioned the smell of lavender, but this wasn't mentioned again when both Jorga and Kylie were found. I have just spoken to Dr Brown, and he has confirmed that there was a slight smell of lavender on both girls most probably from a shampoo or body wash." Looking at the expectant faces of the others in the room "I'll give you one guess what I smelt in Mrs Monroe's bathroom."

"Lavender" they all said together.

"Absolutely right. The other odd thing and I need to ask you ladies this question, how often would you use the loo and leave the seat up." Both confirmed that they would never do that. "That's what I thought, but the toilet seat was up when I used the bathroom." Shrugging "I know in itself, there may be an innocent explanation, but it is strange."

Elaine frowned "I found it very odd that she was so reluctant to provide any contact details for him, so we still don't really know where he is."

"Maybe he's staying with her, that would explain the toilet seat being up." Adam looked perplexed "But if he is why is she so reluctant to tell us, after all their two grown up people so what is there to hide."

"Exactly my thoughts." Elaine added "Thinking about the similarities between all three girls, I just wonder if a quiet chat with Mrs Hole might be in order."

"Just a moment remind me who is Mrs Hole" DCS Collins straightened in his seat.

"She's the school secretary Sir" Elaine leant forward so that she could see everyone clearly "All three girls were from troubled homes, what if there is another child in a similar position. Whoever the perpetrator is they seem to be targeting that school and that type of home environment."

With a quizzical look on his face DCS Collins asked "Right, but what do you suppose we could do with that information. If we step in and place the child and their family under police protection, the perpetrator might just move on to another school or completely disappear for the foreseeable future."

"Could we keep them under surveillance. If the person is going to strike it's most probably going to be sooner rather than later. After all there was only a few days between the others and we're now nearly at a week."

"Okay, I see your point." DCS Collins stroked his chin as he thought through the situation "you speak to Mrs Hole and I'll have a word with Commander Fowler, do not set up any type of operation before I come back to you."

"I'll phone first thing in the morning, Sir." Elaine nodded in agreement.

"Has Dr Brown given you an indication on any progress that Professor Parker is making?" When George confirmed that he had not DCS Collins walked to the door "Good work everyone, keep me informed." With that he was gone.

"Lucky devil" Scott muttered "I could murder a nice roast dinner."

42

The individual wasn't happy as all of their plans had been thrown into disarray. They had chosen the next girl; the nightdress was ready, and the location had been identified. But outside influences were interfering with their timings. These things couldn't be rushed.

"Now I'm going to have to find a local dealer" they scowled "no time to get up and back to London. Why can't people be more considerate and let me work to my plan." Chewing their lip and deep in thought "where can I go that no-one will recognise me, anywhere close by is a complete no-no but I'm going to have to be careful I need that heroin."

Later that night the individual ventured out and made their way to Canchester which is the nearest city to Bournliegh, slowly driving around the back streets they spot a young woman obviously plying her trade.

Stopping the car, the individual winds down the window and shouts across at her. As the girl approaches she stares in disbelief "What do you want? I can't just stand here talking my man will skin my ass."

"Where can I get some decent heroin?" speaking gruffly "and I don't want to be ripped off."

"What's in it for me?" The girl leant on the car as she spoke.

"A tenner, if it's good stuff." Taking the money out of their pocket "you go and get me the gear and bring it back here and this is yours." Waving the note just out of her reach

"and don't go bringing your pimp back to try and rob me" slitting their eyes to look as menacing as possible *"Do you understand, no funny stuff or your mouth will be so swollen that you won't be able to give a blowjob for a month! Now hurry up."* With that the individual closed the car window.

The girl scurried away as fast as her skinny legs would carry her. The individual sat drumming their fingers on the steering wheel impatiently waiting for her to return. Twenty minutes later they heard the click clack of her stupidly high heels as she emerged from the shadows of the alley opposite where the car was parked. Looking around nervously she hurried over to the car, as the window slowly opened she pushed a small bag of heroin into the individual's hand *"£20 for that plus my tenner."* She murmured whilst still looking around.

Thrusting the money at her *"This had better be good, or I'll be back remember I know where to find you."* Closing the window, the individual quickly drove away.

The girl stood watching the car drive away *"I know you from somewhere."* Nodding her head, she walked back towards the alley.

43

Early the following morning Elaine rang Mrs Hole at the school, keeping her fingers crossed that Mrs Monroe wouldn't be able to overhear the conversation. "Good morning Mrs Hole, this is Detective Chief Inspector Edwards, I wonder if I might have an off the record conversation with you please."

"Yes of course, how can I help you." Elaine noticed that the other woman was speaking softly and assumed that the headmistress must be close by.

"Are you able to talk at the moment or should I call back?" when the woman confirmed that it was fine to continue Elaine asked, "this is going to seem like a strange question, but can you think of any other child in the school who you would consider an at-risk child."

"Oh, my goodness Chief inspector I hope that you don't think that I am a gossip or a busy body. I really don't delve into other people's business." The woman sounded quite indignant at the very thought.

Quickly Elaine realised that she needed to get the woman back on side "Not at all Mrs Hole. But if I may talk to you in confidence, your input could prove very valuable to our investigation."

"Well, if you put it like that." The woman's voice softened again "there is one dear little thing that always looks as though she could do with a good wash and a good meal." Sighing "The poor little thing is always by herself at playtime and the others do make fun of her, because she's always a bit on the dirty side and they say that she smells." Without prompting she continued "her mother, or so I'm told is a drug taker and leaves Betsy to fend for herself when she's high."

"Betsy?" Elaine repeated "Betsy, what's her full name and do you have an address for her?"

Elaine could hear the clicking of Mrs Hole's computer keyboard "Betsy Taylor, her mother is Jaqueline Taylor no father is registered with us." The clicking started again "here's the address 16 Valley Road," the woman sounded shocked as she added "Oh dear god, all of them Maggie, Jorga, Kylie and Betsy all live in the same area."

"One other thing, do you happen to have a photograph of Betsy, maybe in a yearbook?" Elaine crossed her fingers and held her breath.

"We should have one as we keep a copy of all of the yearbooks here, just a moment let me check." After a few minutes "Yes, I have one, I'll scan a copy over to you Chief Inspector." Elaine listened as the sound of a photocopier could be heard "done it should be with you shortly. Is there anything else? Only I really must get on."

After thanking Mrs Hole and stressing how important it was that their conversation remained confidential, Elaine hung up the phone and went in search of George.

"Right, that does it, we need to set up surveillance on both the school and the child's home. Are the others in yet?" straightening his tie "I take it that DCS Collins has given the okay."

The next couple of hours were a frenzy of activity, DCS Collins had been given the green light from Commander Fowler to proceed with covert surveillance.

It had been confirmed that Ms. Jaqueline Taylor was a known drug offender and had been arrested on multiple occasions. No-one could understand why she had been allowed to keep Betsy. Her case worker had been spoken to and they were informed that Jaquelines mother lived just outside of Bournliegh, and every time Jaqueline was arrested the mother would take Betsy to stay with her. Unfortunately for the child her grandmother was unable to keep her permanently.

Uniform officers, who had been instructed to wear civvies, together with detectives had been paired up and a shift pattern worked out. Once everyone knew what they were doing the first shift left to take up their positions.

Just as Elaine was about to suggest to George that they grab a quick sandwich her desk phone rang, before she could speak Dr Brown cut in "Elaine, can you come to the mortuary now please it is very important, Professor Parker has found something that you will want to see."

"On my way." Grabbing her jacket from the back of the chair, she didn't need to say anything to George he was already racing across the outer office, pulling on his jacket as he went.

Within twenty minutes both were each dressed in the obligatory white coats and were entering the mortuary.

Looking up Dr Brown indicated for them to join him and a very tall and distinguished looking man next to one of the metal mortuary tables.

"Detectives welcome" holding up his gloved hands Professor Parker continued "I won't shake your hands if you don't mind." Looking down at the covered body on the table "This is Kylie, as I understand she is your third victim." Pulling back the sheet so that Kylie's head and neck could be seen "As you know during the full autopsy that Dr Brown carried out no reason for the child's death could be found." Taking a small torch and a very strong magnifying glass from the nearby table, he shone the torch into Kylie's left ear and peered through the magnifying glass. "If you look here, you will see a very small puncture wound." Handing both items to Elaine "I believe that this child has been injected with a substance that caused her death!"

After Elaine had examined the spot she stepped to one side to allow George to look "Do you have any indication of what it could be?"

"At this moment no, but we now know that we need to look for any poisons that would not normally be covered in an autopsy." Taking the tools back from George, Professor Parker continued "Poisons are not readily available, so unless your killer is a chemist or has chemicals readily available to them, it would be very difficult to come across anything potent enough to kill someone. You would need specialist knowledge of what type of poison to use and the quantity needed."

"Professor Parker has also suggested sending the nightdresses to a colleague that he knows, a specialist in fabrics and the retrieval of fingerprints from most types of fabric." Dr Brown puffed out his cheeks "the nightdresses would of course be sent under very strict conditions to stop any form of contamination."

"Professor Parker, have you found the same mark on Maggie and Jorga?" George shoved his hands in his pockets so that the others couldn't see that his fingers were crossed.

"Indeed, we have" Professor Parker glanced towards the closed mortuary drawers where the two girl's bodies were stored "Now we just need to find out what killed them."

Thanking both Professor Parker and Dr Brown the two detectives made their way back to the station.

Elaine was just about to suggest calling it a night when suddenly the outer office door banged open and both Elaine and George sat open mouthed as a skinny woman in a short tight skirt and sky-high heels tottered towards them "Hi" the woman waved as she walked across to Elaine's office "Detective Constable Donna Deaks, sorry about the gear" looking down at her clothes "just come off a pimp and punter patrol" indicating a chair "do you mind these bloody heels are killing me."

Sitting forward Elaine held her hand out to the woman "DCI Elaine Edwards and this….." indicating towards George "is DCI George Woods. How can we help you?"

"Well ma'am I think that it's me who can help you!" Donna crossed her long legs "My boss, DCI Jordan heard that you are looking for any unusual behaviour that may be connected to the girl's murders."

"You think that you've spotted something?" George who hadn't taken his eyes off of the DC asked.

"It might be nothing, but it just seemed really strange." Looking at the full coffee cup on the desk in front of George "Do you mind?" George handed the cup to her "My patch tonight was a street corner over in the Colebrook area of Canchester, my partner was parked in the alley, we were really after punters but had a stash of substitute heroin in the car." Swallowing some of the hot coffee "Sometimes it's a way to reel the punters in. Anyway, about half an hour before my shift ended a car pulled up and the occupant called me over. I couldn't see their face as they were wearing a hoody and had a scarf pulled up over most of their face. It was very unnerving." Placing the coffee cup back on the desk "Anyway what they wanted was heroin, after doing a bit of haggling I went back to my partner, and he phoned the boss." Looking at both of the detectives "you see I'm sure that it was a woman and I'm convinced that I recognised the voice." Tugging at her skirt that had wriggled up her thighs "I'm sure that I've spoken to her at the school where my son goes, it sounded to me a lot like the headmistress. Anyway, the boss instructed that we should sell the heroin, well the heroin substitute. Obviously we don't go around selling the real stuff, to anyone just to let you know."

"Does your son attend Longmead Primary?" Elaine was trying to digest what the DC had just told them.

"Yes, that's right. We also ran the car registration number, but it turned out to be a rental car. The guy there told my boss that it had been rented out to a Mr Ruiz and its due back at their car lot tomorrow morning."

As the woman stood up Elaine stated, "Thank you so much and thank DCI Jordan for me." Elaine smiled as she looked at George watching the woman wriggle her way across the outer office "Okay, tongues back in mouth please." Quickly adding "Right we need a car staking out the car lot first thing tomorrow." Tapping her fingers on the desk she asked, "Should we have Mrs Monroe brought in?"

"If it was her in the car, she will want to get those drugs to Mrs Taylor tomorrow." Seeing the frown on Elaine's face "think about it, she wants Mrs Taylor out of the way when Betsy comes out of school, so the best way for that is for the mother to be as high as a kite."

"How do you think that she'll get the drugs to her. She can hardly walk up to the woman and give them to her!" Elaine's frown deepened.

"No, she can't but I bet my police pension that she'll use a courier." George looked longingly at his now empty coffee cup "that's what I would do!"

"Okay, so surveillance on the car lot and the same on the Taylor's home." Stopping for a moment "No, on second thoughts we need to get Mrs Taylor away from the house and have a police officer take control of any package that's delivered." George agreed and they started to work on getting the plan together ready for action early the following morning.

44

The individual had found a parking spot that allowed them to watch from a distance as the courier knocked on the door of 16 Valley Road. After what seemed forever the door was cracked open slightly and a small package was handed over.

From where they were sitting the individual couldn't see who had taken the package, but all they were concerned about was that it had been delivered. Putting their car in gear they pulled off and drove towards the town center.

Looking at their watch they estimated that they had plenty of time to drive out to the lockup change cars and be back in time to intercept Betsy on her way home from school. They had calculated that her mother would be out of it for the rest of the day and most of the night from the amount of heroin that they had sent her.

If they had only waited for a couple more minutes they would have seen Detective Constable Chambers exit the house with the package in an evidence bag.

Smiling with the anticipation of what the day would bring, they continued on their journey totally oblivious to the fact that their world was crumbling around them.

45

"We have the package, ma'am" Adam spoke into his mobile "patrol has just taken the parcel and are on their way over to the lab."

"Great, thank you" Elaine breathed a sigh of relief "I've just heard from PC Susie Blake that she's making sure Mrs Taylor is staying out of sight at the hotel. Keep me informed Adam." Signing off she turned to where George was sitting staring at a computer screen showing all of the different angles from the Bournliegh CCTV system. "Any luck?"

"Not yet." Picking up his coffee cup "Haven't spotted a van matching the description that Mr Ahmed gave us. Lots of cars moving up and down the estate roads but can't see anything suspicious." The next few hours seemed to drag by with no news.

"I want to be near the school when Betsy comes out" Elaine stated, "If anything goes wrong ………..."

"Come on let's go, I'd feel better if we were out in the field and not sitting here on our backsides, if we leave now we'll beat the parents, before they nick all of the parking spaces." George held the door open for Elaine seeing the surprise on her face "I know it's not politically correct but I'm too old to care about all this new-fangled bollocks."

Parking up they sat in silence, as the parents started to arrive they both pretended to be looking at their mobiles to avoid looking suspicious. The school bell rang at exactly 3.00

pm, but to their surprise instead of Mrs Monroe coming out to unlock the gate it was Mr Austin.

Opening her mobile Elaine quickly dialed a number after introducing herself she asked "Mrs Hole, is Mrs Monroe still in the school" George couldn't hear what the other woman said but looking at his colleagues face it wasn't good "What! She hasn't been in all day. Is she sick?" again silence "Okay, thank you."

"For Christ's sake, haven't you ever thought about putting your phone on speaker." George glared across at Elaine "What's happened?"

"She, Mrs Monroe didn't turn up for school today and no-one can get hold of her." Dialing another number "Ted, get a patrol car round to Mrs Monroe's home immediately please. Get them to look through all the windows try the doors; I need to know urgently if she's there."

Just as she finished the call George nudged her "Isn't that Betsy?"

"Yes" glancing down the row of parked cars to where a woman had just stepped out from one of them, Elaine nodded "and that's PC Cooper. Good girl she could pass as a mum any day."

Watching as PC Cooper walked slowly, so that she wouldn't draw any attention to herself and staying on the opposite side of the road to Betsy she carefully followed the little girl.

As soon as they rounded the corner George started the engine and was just about to pull out when a white van roared past "What the hell!" George exploded "Bloody idiot." Hesitating he shouted "No, I'm the bloody idiot" pulling out quickly he raced after the van, as they turned the corner the van had disappeared. "Where's the kid." Both looked frantically up and down all of the side roads but couldn't see any sign of either Betsy or PC Cooper.

"There, there" Elaine shouted, "Cut through, I bet she normally takes a short cut home." Breathing heavily "quick get round to the end of the lane, I bet that's where the van's waiting."

PC Case was standing, half hidden, at the exit of the cut-through watching the girl, as she made her way up Brockhurst Road in the direction of Valley Road. Stepping out from the shadow of the bushes that covered the exit to the lane, she was about to cross the road when a white van turned the corner into the road. As the van approached PC Case it seemed to slow down and then drove at speed past where Betsy was waiting to cross the road and disappeared out of sight.

As soon as Betsy had safely entered her home, PC Case pulled her mobile from her pocket "Ma'am, Betsy home safe and well." Pausing "Ma'am something strange happened. I'm sure that the van we are looking for drove past me, sorry but I couldn't get the number plate as it was covered with what looked like mud." Listening for a moment she continued "I think that the person in the van recognised me, as they slowed down as they approached me and then quickly sped away."

Elaine looked at George who had parked the car whilst listening to what the PC had to say. Leaving the phone on hands free she quickly dialed a number "Ted, is the patrol car still at Mrs Monroe's home now please. If she's not there can they check when any of her neighbours last saw her. Ted put me through to control will you." Thanking the Sergeant, she waited to be connected "Good Afternoon, this is DCI Edwards please issue a BOLO, (Be On The Look Out), for a Mrs Betty Monroe, I'm sending you her vehicle details. I also need Bristol Airport security to be watching for her." Finishing the call, she quickly dialed DCS Collins number "Sir, we think that the perpetrator is Mrs Monroe, I have asked for a BOLO to be issued including the airport."

"Right, but I would have liked to have been told before you started issuing orders DCI Edwards!" DCS Collins gruff voice barked down the phone.

"Sorry sir, but I thought that it was imperative that we get everyone looking for her as soon as possible. Especially as we missed the opportunity of finding Mr Ruiz at the car lot this morning."

"Okay, well let's hope that you're right. Keep me informed." DCS Collins added "Immediately, if you don't mind!"

46

The individual spotted Betsy as they drove around the corner into Brockhurst Road. She had walked about halfway down the road heading towards her home. Smiling the individual started to follow her when suddenly they caught sight of a woman emerging from the cut through that Betsy had taken. Racking their brains, the individual tried to place where they had seen the woman before. When suddenly it came to them, and they nearly choked as they spat out the words "Bloody hell she's a police officer." Angrily they tightened their grip on the steering wheel "I need to get out of here." They muttered to themselves as they sped up the road and passed the little girl who had been their target today.

Driving as fast as they could without breaking any speed limits the individual headed for home.

"I must be careful if they're on to me they may be at the house." The individual spoke out loud to themselves as they drove. "What to do next? I need to get some clothes and my passport before anyone can stop me."

As the individual got nearer to their cul-de-sac they found a parking spot and decided that it might be safer to walk to the corner to see if they could spot any suspicious vehicles near their house. Making sure that no-one else was around they made their way along the road and standing with their back against a wall they slowly peaked around the corner into the cul-de-sac. Quickly ducking down behind a parked car, as the individual watched as a police patrol car pulled out of the road.

"Christ that was close!" breathing heavily they made their way quickly into the cul-de-sac. Once inside the house it only took a few minutes to throw a few things into a bag and grab their important documents. A quick call to the airline as they hurried back to the van, stashing their bag on the passenger seat they drove off towards the airport.

Elaine and George made their way to Valley Road and pulled into a parking spot a few houses from the Taylors home. As they got out of the car and started to make their way towards the house a woman called to them from across the street "At last, you lot have taken your time!"

Both Detectives looked across at the woman "Excuse me madam" Elaine noticed that George was using his polite voice "What exactly do you mean?"

Pointing to the Taylors house the woman replied "Like I say about bloody time someone takes that poor little bugger away from that stupid drugged up bitch. Poor little thing looks like she could do with a good wash and a decent meal."

"If you don't mind me asking have you ever bothered to report this issue, madam." His tone had now changed from being polite to full on sarcastic.

Scowling the woman shrugged "None of my business."

"Exactly right." George firmly stated, "Now be on your way, nothing for you to see here."

Trying hard to suppress a smile Elaine whispered "Well, that told her."

Adam Chambers stood at the open front door watching the exchange, "Everything alright ma'am." he asked as they approached him.

As Elaine was about to respond to Adam, her mobile phone started to ring "Detective Chief Inspector Edward."

"Ma'am, I've just heard from Bristol Airport, Mrs Monroe has just booked a ticket for the 7.30 flight to Alicante tonight." The control operator's line crackled as they spoke.

Thanking them Elaine indicated to George to join her as she punched a number into her phone "Good Afternoon Sir, we have just had confirmation that Mrs Monroe is flying out to Alicante tonight. Can I have your permission to make an arrest."

"Just get there before the flight takes off, we can't afford any mistakes." He paused "I'll send back up but instruct no blues and two's and that no-one enters the airport building without your say so, we don't want to alert the perpetrator."

"We're on our way." Elaine gave George a thumbs up "The airport please and don't spare the horses."

The journey to the airport took nearly an hour, although it seemed like a lifetime to Elaine. As they pulled into the airport causeway Elaine phoned through to airport security to confirm if Mrs Monroe was in the building, they told her that they had eyes on the lady, and she was at present waiting in line for baggage control to open.

Making their way through the crowds of people who were milling around inside the building Elaine and George finally recognised Mrs Monroe. George looked at Elaine and smiling said "Go on this is your arrest."

Quietly making her way past the other passengers who were waiting in line for baggage control, Elaine stood behind Mrs Monroe "Mrs Betty Monroe." As the startled woman turned to face Elaine she continued "or should I say Mr Trevor

Monroe. I am arresting you for the murders of Maggie Burnett, Jorga O'Brien and Kylie Smith. You do not have to say anything, but it may harm your defense if you do not mention when questioned something that you later rely on in court. Anything that you do say may be given in evidence. Do you understand the caution.?"

    By the time that Elaine and George had driven back to the station, the custody Sergeant told them that Mr Monroe requested a lawyer. Unfortunately, the lawyer was unavailable until the following morning. Mr Monroe was subsequently placed in a cell within the custody suite. The Sergeant also confirmed that Mr Monroe's clothes at the time of his arrest had been placed in evidence bags. These consisted of a woman's wig and several items of women's clothing.

48

The following morning Elaine and George regrouped to once again go over the information that they had compiled the previous night. This was in readiness for the interview with Mr Monroe and his solicitor.

Along with both their own team of detectives and uniformed officers assisted by Dr Brown and the forensic science team they had all worked tirelessly overnight to gather as much evidence as possible.

Last night DCS Collins had spoken to his counterpart in the Spanish Guarda who had promised that an immediate search of Mrs Monroe's villa would be carried out as a matter of urgency.

At precisely 10.30 am Elaine was informed that Mr Monroe and his solicitor were waiting for them in interview room 2. Looking out into the outer office Elaine signaled to George that they were ready, as she walked across to where he was standing he held out his hand, seeing confusion on her face he explained "It's one of my traditions before going into a murder interview I always shake hands with the other detective" shrugging he smiled "I know but humour me!"

As they entered interview room 2 Elaine was surprised to see such a young solicitor sitting next to Mr Monroe, she had expected one of the older more experienced solicitors to act on such an important case. As the two detectives took their seats on the opposite side of the table, Elaine pressed the button on the machine to start recording the interview "The date is October 9th, 2023, the time 10.36 am. Present are Detective Chief Inspector Elaine Edwards."

George added "Detective Chief Inspector George Wood."

Mr Monroe's solicitor indicated to his client to speak "Trevor Monroe." After which the solicitor introduced himself "Mr Roger Haskin."

Elaine started "Mr Monroe although you were cautioned yesterday I would like to repeat this for the tape." When she had reaffirmed the caution "do you understand." Mr Monroe replied that he understood.

"Before you go any further Detective Chief Inspector I would like it to be known that my client has prepared a statement which I will read to you: -

I, Trevor Monroe, have no knowledge or any information with regard to the murder of Maggie Burnett, Jorga O'Brien or Kylie Smith. To my knowledge I have never met these young girls and therefore have nothing else to add in connection with the police enquiries into their murders.

The solicitor slid a copy of the statement across to Elaine as he added "Therefore I have advised my client to remain silent during this interview."

Elaine moved the copy statement to one side "Thank you, however we do have a lot to present to your client." Opening one of the many files that the two detectives had brought into the interview room and looking directly at Mr Monroe "Overnight we have had a team of highly skilled investigators at your home, they are still there at present. We have received some very good information from them" taking a photograph from the open file she pushed it across the table "this sewing machine has been removed and is now with the crime lab, we believe that the nightdresses that the girls were found in was made on this machine." Seeing a small smile twitch at the corner of the man's lips she added "you see every machine has a different stitch pattern, a little like humans have fingerprints. Speaking of which several fingerprints have been found within the home which are being compared to each of the girl's fingerprints."

On seeing that the man appeared to be slightly uncomfortable with this information George quickly added "We also have your white van and both of your cars."

"How the hell did you ………" Mr Monroe shouted before his solicitor could stop him.

George continued "Your van was picked up on CCTV earlier yesterday and one of our fine undercover officers followed you to the out-of-town lockup." Glancing at Elaine "it's strange that nobody ever seems to notice motor bikes!" shaking his head slightly "Your lockup is a treasure trove of very valuable evidence. Detective Chief Inspector Edwards would you mind sharing the photographs from the lockup with Mr Monroe and his solicitor please." Several photographs were slid across the table "as you can see, we discovered a bale of white linen material which is now being compared to the nightdresses, a passport and driving license in the name of Alejo Ruiz, who looks remarkably like you." With that George sat back in his chair and watched as both the solicitor and Mr Monroe digested this information "However, I believe that my colleague has further information for you."

"Indeed" Elaine opened another file "Whilst searching your home, our officers found these" pushing two more photographs across the table "as you will see a white nightdress, similar to the one's that Maggie, Jorga and Kylie were dressed in was found along with a hand written note that read 'ninguna energia de parar' which we believe means 'no power to stop' were you referring to Mrs Taylor not being able to stop taking drugs or to yourself not being able to stop murdering young girls."

"Now really I must object I believe that you are goading my client and I think that now would be a very good time to take a break." Although the solicitor was trying to muster as much bravado as possible he seemed resigned to the fact that the evidence was overwhelming.

"Of course, we can take a break if that's what you want Mr Haskin, but before we do I would just like to share one more piece of evidence with your client." Elaine straightened up in her seat "The package that you thought was heroin" pausing for effect "or should I say the heroin substitute that you sent to Mrs Taylor was purchased from an undercover officer and instead of being delivered to Mrs Taylor we had a detective at her house who took control of the delivery."

"I'm not sure how you will present that in court Detective Chief Inspector, unless your officer identified my client at point of sale." The solicitor smiled as he spoke.

"Fingerprints on the bag containing the powder confirm that your client handled the said bag. Interview suspended at 11.40 am." Noticing the smile slide off the solicitor's face Elaine and George stood and left the room.

As they walked out of the room they were greeted with the sight of Scott rushing towards them "Ma'am" breathing heavily "DCS Collins wants to see you both immediately." Catching his breath "it must be important he told me to interrupt your interview."

After thanking Scott, the two detectives made their way up the stairs to DCS Collins office where they were immediately ushered into the room by his secretary "Sir, you wanted to see us." Elaine and George stood in front of the big oak desk where the DCS was seated.

"Sit down for god's sake" DCS Collins indicated the chairs opposite him "I've heard back from Spain." Steepling his fingers "they have conducted a search of the villa but there appeared to be no sign of Mrs Monroe." As George was about to speak the DCS stopped him "but as they were about to leave one of the neighbours approached them, apparently the locals have suspected for a long time that something untoward had happened to Mrs Monroe. This particular neighbour told the Guarda that some years ago Mr Monroe had hired a mini digger from a local firm. Just after that the neighbour noticed that a big new flower bed had been built at the edge of the property, at the time he thought it was a strange place to have a flower bed but put it down to an English idiosyncrasy, but now he's wondering if it could have been built for a more sinister reason."

Elaine gasped "Do they think that Mrs Monroe is buried there?"

"They can't say that at present, but they are going to excavate to be sure one way or the other." DCS Collins frowned "What I want you to do is to casually drop some hints about Mrs Monroe, see what sort of reaction you get." When both detectives confirmed this "Right get back to it, let's hope that this new information will rattle his cage!"

Walking back down the stairs towards the interview room Elaine felt as though they were at a breakthrough point. As they re-entered the room the solicitor's face paled as he seemed to recognize that the situation had changed.

Once the recording had been started again Elaine looked directly at Mr Monroe and asked, "Can you tell us the reason for you being dressed and acting as your wife prior to your arrest? When Elaine received no reply she continued "Can you tell us where your wife is?

Mr Monroe looked at his solicitor before answering "I think that you mean my ex-wife! How would I know where she is, she doesn't have to answer to me."

"But surely as you seem to be staying at her home you would have some idea of where we might find her." Elaine put her head to one side "Oh! Sorry I just assumed that the men's clothes that we found at the house was yours, are you trying to tell us that she has another man staying there?"

"Don't be so bloody disgusting" the man almost spat the words back at Elaine.

"What's so disgusting, as you have rightly pointed out she is your ex-wife so if she wants to have another man in her life it's nothing to do with you." Elaine smiled as she spoke.

"I really must protest………" the pale faced solicitor started to speak only to be cut off by Elaine.

"So where is she?" Elaine pronounced every word carefully.

"At the bloody villa, that's where she'll be" the man was now red faced with anger "loves that bloody villa more than life itself. That's where she'll be."

Just as Elaine was about to answer Scott knocked on the door and slowly opened it to ask Elaine if he could have a word. George announced for the tape that DCI Edwards had left the room and then sat looking at the two men across the table in silence.

After five minutes Elaine came back into the room and after confirming, for the tape, that she had re-entered the room she proceeded to speak "You are quite right our colleagues in the Guarda have confirmed that Mrs Monroe is at the villa as you rightly stated." Looking straight into Mr Monroes eyes she continued "well what I should say is that your ex-wife isn't at the villa but is actually in the flower bed." Seeing the colour drain from the man's face "they have confirmed that a body has been recovered from the flower bed at the edge of the garden, which neighbours have confirmed seeing you build." Pausing just for a moment "We understand that the Spanish police will be sending someone to the UK to speak to you with regard to this matter."

Chapter 49

It was a cold wet Sunday morning as DCI Edwards and DCI Woods sat in Elaine's office at Bournleigh police station. Neither DCI had managed to get much sleep the night before as both felt that they needed to tie up the loose ends that was still bothering them about the case.

Elaine flipped open one of the files, that was piled on the desk between them. She slid out the photograph of the group of children in year 3, that had been found on the desk in the corner of Mr Monroes sitting room. Placing the photograph so that both could see it she asked, "The thing that is bothering me is why those particular girls?" turning the photograph slightly she pointed to a young boy in the second row "That is Tommy Jones, his father is a renowned drunk and is always being pulled in for drunk and disorderly conduct. So why take Maggie and not him?"

George looked straight at Elaine "Why take a boy that might fight, when you can take a little girl who could be easier to control."

Leaning forward again Elaine pointed to another child "Okay I get your point, but this one is Emily Broad." She pointed to a petite little dark-haired girl sitting next to Jorga in the front row. "Her father is a prolific burglar and is at present sitting in jail. So again, why try to take Kylie and not Emily?" Without waiting for George to answer she pointed to yet another child "This is Christina May; her father is a meth user. Social services can't be sure if her stepmother uses meth as well, but apparently the house is a right state, and their social worker is on the brink of taking Christina into foster care.

"Blimey, so many children either at risk or potentially at risk in one year group it's nearly unbelievable." George leaned back in this chair deep in thought after a moment he suddenly said, "I think I know why." Running a hand through his hair "Think about it Elaine, all of the girls that were taken were from one parent families, right." Elaine nodded her agreement "but the one parent was a mother!"

"Oh my god you're right" rubbing a hand over her face "these others live with their fathers or in Emily's case father and stepmother."

"Exactly, so if for any reason a situation arose Mr Monroe was convinced that he could overpower a mother but not a father, that's why these particular girls were targeted." George looked down at the photograph "the next question is if he hadn't been stopped would he have gone after any others."

"Let's just be grateful that he was caught, and all of these other children won't be another victim." Elaine picked up her coffee cup and took a sip, pulling a face at the now cold content of the cup.

"I still don't get why the white nightdresses; do you think that they symbolise something from his past?" as he spoke George reached over and picked up Elaines cup "Want a fresh one?"

As George walked across to the small office kitchen, Elaine opened another file and started to study the photographs of how the young girls were found. Looking from Maggie to Jorga and then Kylie, suddenly something clicked.

"Dear lord, how thick are we." She stated as George, two coffee cups in hand, walked back into the office. Without waiting for the man to speak Elaine hurriedly explained "White nightdresses, babies are normally clothed in white. A baby in the womb is in a foetal position. Right?" George nodded "My god, I bet the one thing that he wanted and couldn't have was a child of his own."

"So, seeing these, in his mind disgraceful mothers, a drunk, a thief, a prostitute and a drug taker, with these beautiful girls sent him over the edge." George frowned "Do you think that was the reason that Mrs Monroe died, because she wouldn't or couldn't give him a child." Elaine nodded "You know you could be right." Pausing "But we still don't know how he killed them. For me that's the strangest part, other than the small puncture mark inside the girls ears, no poisons were found during autopsies and there were no other wounds found on them, so how the hell did he do it?"

Shaking her head "We have had the best of the best examine the bodies and if they can't find the answer to that, then I don't think that we will ever know."

With that the two DCIs walked out of the building to enjoy what was left of their Sunday.

Printed in Great Britain
by Amazon